Secret of the Seeds

Kate Muus

First Hedgehog & Fox Edition, May 2015

This is a work of fiction. Names, characters, places, and incidents either are the product of the author's imagination or are used fictitiously. Any resemblance to actual persons, living or dead, events, or locals is entirely coincidental.

Library of Congress has catalogued the Hedgehog & Fox edition as follows:
Muus, Kate
Heirloom / Kate Muus. - 1st ed.
p. cm.
1. Insurgency — Fiction. 2. Survival — Fiction. 3. Interpersonal relations — Fiction.
4. New Adult — Fiction. 5. Secrets — Fiction. 6. Seeds — Fiction

ISBN: 978-0-9961950-4-1
eISBN: 978-0-9961950-5-8

Cover design by Frances Parker. Special Font, Gloss Drop, by phospho.

More information can be learned about Hedgehog & Fox at warnerliterarygroup.com

Printed in the United States of America.

To Rob
All my everything, always.

To my boys
At the end of your days,
when someone asks, "What did you do?"
be able to say, "All that I could."

Proverbs 11:26

"The people curse him who holds back grain, but a blessing is on the head of him who sells it."

Cane pulled the manure sack from the top of the spreader and wiped his forehead with the back of his yellow work glove. He snarled his lip. He sniffed loudly and hocked spit into the dirt. It was dusk and he was finished, except for the sowing. There was a continual bend in his knee as he walked. His jeans were brown with fertilized fields; his white tank a stark contrast to his raisin skin. His hair grew down to his shoulders and greyed at the temples, while the rest lay black. His body was narrow; he was strong. He walked towards the amber light of the blue farmhouse to a figure in white.

She was young, only seventeen, a brunette with long hair and light eyes. When he got within a few yards of her he stopped, leaned on his hip.

"Who the hell are you?" More sniffing. More spit. He rested his weight on the opposite hip.

She wasn't surprised. She hardly reacted. "It's me, Uncle Cane. It's Ceres." She held her summer hat in front of her white skirt. The hat was made of straw and had a big black bow on its front. It matched her wedged heels with likened black bows. She looked like she belonged in a picture of the farmhouse from the 40s.

Cane stood staring then started to shake his head. The shaking became more vigorous as he started into the house. "Aster! Aster," he shouted and stormed up the wooden farmhouse stairs.

Ceres followed him inside, a few steps behind. He let the door slam on her before she came in.

The two-story farmhouse had a wraparound porch, painted white but cracked and weathered. It smelled like lavender and dust on the inside as Ceres walked into the front room.

"Aster! Where are ya? Aster?" He went through the front room, through the swinging doors to the kitchen as the young girl followed and the wood floors beneath them creaked. "This ain't gonna work," he said as the old woman slid a bottle across the counter to him.

"Now, now" she rasped, "what are you ravin' about Cane?"

Ceres floated through the swinging doors into the kitchen. "Auntie Aster!" she said, hugging her feeble frame. The small woman was enveloped in Ceres's arms, and her short dark hair was in Ceres's face.

Aster barely held herself there. "Oh, Ceres! Oh, Ceres you're here. You're finally here."

"*This* is what I'm talkin' 'bout Aster. *This* ain't gonna work." He eyed her up and down again then went to sit down in his recliner, facing away from the women to drink his beer.

Ceres ignored his complaint and said, "I'm so happy to see you, Auntie Aster. I almost thought I'd be too late." Aster looked worried, and quickly took Ceres's hat from her and placed it on the light green kitchen counter.

"No worry, dear. You are just in time." She tried to smile, but her eyes did more talking than her thin lips.

"I mean it, Aster. Not gonna work," Cane's words spit towards the TV in the living room. He took a long swig of his beer.

"Let's go to your room, your new room," Aster said shuffling Ceres out the swinging door to the downstairs hallway. "You'll be right next to me, an' Cane sleeps upstairs now when he manages the strength to get off the recliner." She whimpered a laugh and Ceres smiled, remembering the loud laugh that Aster boasted in her youth.

"Are you sure I can stay?" Ceres asked, referring to Cane's refusal.

"Uncle Cane'll just have to get used to ya. He hasn't been around you kids in so long. An' after your cousin, well, he didn't see much use in keepin' kids around." Aster looked away from her.

Ceres's cousin, Erving, had been an invalid. He was a disappointment to Cane from birth, who was so excited to have a strong boy of his own on the farm. The help would be born into the family. There'd be no need to pay someone from the outside.

When Aster had him, the fear that it could be a girl was relieved but matched with equal disappointment when he came out with a crippled hand. And that was the end of it. He stayed inside with Aster until he was 18, then he went away. Ceres wasn't sure if he went to college or to another country; she wasn't sure if Aster and Cane knew either. He never came back. Cane always blamed Aster for his son's *inadequacies,* said she was *broken.*

Ceres looked up from her suitcase and said quite seriously, "Aunt Aster, I'm seventeen years old."

"An' already a graduate to boot!" Aster added. "I know you're all grown. But Cane an' me will always see you as the little girl playin' in the fountain at the Foundry Park in the city." She softened her voice and said, "I'm sorry abou' your graduation. I wanted so much for someone to be there, someone from your family. I just couldn't make the two trips out after..."

Her voice trailed off. She knew Aster meant the funeral. Ceres fingered the pages of a book on the fireplace mantle across from the bed, "I know."

Aster whispered, "They're angels you know."

Ceres breathed in deeply, and cocked her head to the side. She bent over to undo the clips of her shoes. "Thank you for taking me in. I know it's not easy with the farm. I'll earn my keep."

"It's only for a few months, until you're 18. Then you can go off to college, where were you accepted again?" Aster asked.

Ceres knew she couldn't afford it after paying her parents' funeral costs and hospital bills. She'd only stay until she turned 18 in September, then she'd have to make it on her own somehow.

"Damn right you'll earn your keep," Cane said from the doorway. He leaned on one side, beer in hand and took a large swig. Ceres looked up sharply and paused in her undressing. "Don't let me stop you. Yer feet even lay flat against the floor after wearin' those things?"

Ceres unlatched the last clip and stood defiantly on the wooden floor in front of him as if to say *clearly*. "One would have to change their entire genetic makeup to have their feet mold to the shape of a shoe."

Cane scoffed and sauntered back down the hallway, "Damn fancy pants education wearing high-heel hooker shoes."

"They're cute, honey. Pay him no mind."

"I don't," she said placing them under the corner chair and then closing the door. "My mom loved these shoes. She helped me pick them out."

"Well your mom always had the best taste. Best taste in men too. If only I'd been given just a little bit of that taste maybe I'da been a city girl." Her voice quieted again, as if she were telling secrets. Aster took Ceres's right hand. "Your dad had some good taste too," she said holding the gold ring on Ceres's index finger between her own pointer and thumb.

"Yeah," Ceres said holding her hand out in front of her. "He bought this for her in Ireland—on one of his business trips."

"It's upside-down," Aster frowned.

"That means that my heart hasn't been taken, Auntie," she smiled. Aster smiled back. Her niece was whimsical, like her sister had been.

"You wait 'til the best one comes round. Don't you settle for anythin' less." Ceres couldn't help but feel that Aster thought she, herself, had settled.

After she'd unpacked a few of her things, Ceres met Aster in the kitchen to help her with dinner.

"You're a guest, dear," she said. "Just si'down and I'll tell ya when it's ready." She smiled and indicated the sofa chair situated next to Cane's recliner.

"I *wish* she was just a guest," Cane said under his breath from the other room.

"I'd rather help you out, Aunt Aster," she said timidly.

Aster knew the unspoken discomfort and handed her the snap peas while she cut potatoes. "Wash these please. Wash'em good."

Ceres picked up the snap peas and placed them in the silver colander from the countertop. Aster worked on the island that jetted out from the wall and separated the dining table and the living room from the kitchen. Ceres dipped the colander in the running sink water for a moment and then shook it out again, creating a small shower of clear beads before turning the water off.

"Longer, Ceres. You've got to wash each one," Aster scolded as she came over and turned the water back on again, taking the snap pea in her hand and rubbing it with two fingers under the water. She placed each one on a paper towel before moving onto the next. Then she handed the task back to Ceres. "Nothin's worth doin' if you don't do it right." She furrowed her brow. Ceres felt uncomfortable. She held her breath at the back of her throat. Aster quickly tried to comfort her. "Your mom and I used to love to eat snap peas. It'd make Granddad so angry! We would go out to the garden out back and eat'em right off the stalk." She stood for a moment and then, as if she had remembered her sister's death, started rigorously scrubbing the dirt off the potatoes again. She rubbed so hard that she scratched off the skin, leaving little speckles of brown refuse in the sink. She wiped the back of her hand on her brow and coughed severely into the opposite arm.

Her room was at the front of the house, facing the fields. It had been Erving's old room. He was a few years older than Ceres. The mahogany backboard of the bed was perfectly matched with the navy blue bedspread and sheets. There were ceramic bunnies and squirrels everywhere with cartoonish painted eyes. It was as if Aster had placed them there to intentionally try and soften the look of the overly boyish room.

Ceres opened the closet timidly, just to ensure that there wasn't anyone hiding in it. She had been warned that Cane wouldn't like her poking around in things that weren't hers. *If it isn't yours, don't touch it,* Aster warned. Ceres knew it was meant to protect her. The room didn't have his physical being, but it did have material manifestations of Erving. He had left all of his things from his childhood in the closet. He'd never come back for his comic books or the ship he made out of balsam wood on the fireplace mantle.

Ceres slipped herself in between the cotton sheets that felt like starched flax. She opened the drawer next to her twin bed, where she had put her mother's fancy brush, pulled it out and ran it through her mouse brown hair. The plastic made a noise; a dull scratch as the bristles pulled it from its place in the handle. She shut off the light on the nightstand and hunched down farther into the sheets, but not without the uncomfortable fear that there might be spiders in the deepest pockets. She warmed her feet, passing them one over the other. She faced the window that let in a muffled howl of the wind over the farm and shut her eyes. The night was black and there were no stars.

Ceres's eyes popped open at the sound of boots thumping across the ceiling, on the floor above, then rolled back underneath her covers. The thuds ceased and her door pushed open.

"Little lady, you'd better get up," Aster whispered from the hallway. Her voice took a serious tone as Ceres flapped the quilt over to the side. "Ceres…"

The thuds faded down the hallway and then seemed to tumble down the stairs. Ceres's heart sped to the rate of the tumble.

"Where is she? Aster..." His voice was like that of an angry dog snarling as he approached.

Aster met him in the hall, moving him towards the kitchen with some promise of breakfast. Ceres quickly dressed in jeans, a t-shirt and an old pair of tennis shoes and met them in the kitchen. Cane looked up from his meal, which he hovered over like a starved animal—domesticated, he used a fork and knife.

"I'm ready, Uncle Cane," she said through her sleep.

"The hell you are!" he laughed, slurping the last of his coffee from his mug. "Aster'll get ready and you'll follow. Take mental notes. Don't forget any inch of her movements. If you need to make room in your head, just get rid of whatever it was you studied at that fancy private school. It's not important here, darlin'."

Ceres hated that this was her new life—but she had no other choice, no better choice.

Aster was a failing machine. She would sputter and cough, fall over and trip up in her steps. These were not the movements that Cane wanted remembered—or perhaps he did, so that she would know that the roof over her head depended on her efficacy on the land.

While Aster and Ceres bent over chicken coops, Ceres admired the pink and spotted brown eggs, but quickly scuttled away when one of the chickens approached her. Aster laughed at her quietly. Cane tended to the fields—which he referred to as "men's work" in the most predictable way. No need for women in the field, though he could not maintain the acreage by himself. He had a helper, a farmhand named Bry. He was plain and nondescript. He faded in and out of the cornfields as easily as the wind.

By the afternoon, Ceres's feet would ache. Her flesh was hot to the very bone and she swore she could feel her skin bubbling off of her body. Aster claimed it was because her skin was fair and "needed used to" the sun. A hard day's work would do her good, and her skin would toughen up like *leather*.

When Aster said this, Ceres imagined peeling off her skin and handing it over to be made into a couch or purse and parceled off to be sold in the city. She imagined entire stores dedicated to the odd delicacies and shuttered at the thought. Still, she wondered if her leather skin would be soft or stiff.

She quickly asked if they could go into town to buy sunscreen.

Aster said "yes" in the way parents do when they have no idea how they're going to pay for something but would never imagine their child to go without.

They hardly saw Cane all day—which was nice. Ceres felt like it was just her and Aster in the barn, in the farmhouse. She imagined this was what her mom felt as she was growing up at the farmhouse. She would always talk about sisters and how much fun they had at the farm. The pride from growing your own food, the knowledge you were doing something good for the Earth and her people. She tried to think of this every time she felt her shoes rub against her skin or her sunburnt skin burst in anger. It had only been a few months since she had seen her face and somehow she felt close to her mother here.

At the end of the day, after a brief reprieve for lunch, Ceres was ready for it to end but uneager to see her uncle at the house.

"I'll just walk around and make myself familiar with everything, if that's okay?"

Aster knowingly agreed, although that would leave her without help making dinner. She was used to it. She gave Ceres a look as to say, *Don't be found where you don't belong.*

"Twenty minutes, tops," Ceres smiled.

Aster nodded and hobbled back the twenty yards from the barn to the house.

Ceres waited until she was halfway there before sneaking to the other side of the barn. Her back met the siding and she let herself slide down to the dirt. She closed her eyes.

She thought about going to college, about apartments and girlfriends, classes that she might dread and cute biology professors she could dream about marrying. It seemed like such a distant possibility now. After her father died, she finished high school for his memory and paid her boarding school debt with what little money he left her after his medical bills were paid. Money: she now knew she could not ignore.

She liked to think of her father meeting her mother in heaven. She started to hum a melody from her childhood, something her mother used to sing when she herself was upset. It was a melody that calmed her down, off the edge of lunacy; it seemed to have the same effect on Ceres, though she often couldn't remember the words

A shadow fell over her face. "Move," it said.

She peeked open one eye. It was Bry. She was relieved it wasn't Cane. Bry was in his twenties, or he may have been closer to her age. His skin was weathered by years on the farm making it impossible to tell.

"Excuse me?" she couldn't help herself or her manners. No one would be pushing her around, or at least she'd only be pushed around by Cane—no one else.

"Sorry. Move yourself, please. My shovel goes there."

Ceres looked at the entire length of the barn, all available to place his shovel.

"Right here?" she asked in disbelief.

"Yep. Right there."

"Ridiculous," she breathed getting up.

"Actually, it goes inside. Inside the barn."

"Oh, that's nice," she said dusting off her bottom and heading back to the house.

"Dinner," he said.

Ceres didn't turn around.

Ceres moved her feet from a bucket of ice into the steaming hot wash basin in the downstairs' bathroom.

Aster chuckled, which quickly turned to coughing. "Dear, I'm not sure you're cut out for hard labor."

Ceres smiled through the pain. "Look at my lobster feet, Aunt Aster! If I can deal with this I can do anything!"

"You've got your mother's delicate nature," she said. Ceres thought it may have been a compliment, maybe not.

She sat on the edge of the tub and examined the dingy walls. Aster kept it clean, but it was old and the caulking had greyed.

"You shouldn't be working so hard, I'm here to help."

"I'm afraid you'll be here to replace me if things keep going the way they are."

Ceres was startled, "Why do you say that?"

Aster corrected herself, "I say that because you're such a hard worker. Surely Cane will see your hard work. I'll go finish dinner. Ten minutes, okay pumpkin?"

As Ceres came around the hallway corner to the kitchen she saw Cane and Bry sitting at the table. Suddenly Bry's cryptic "dinner" message made sense. She feigned a comfortable gait as she came into the room and sat in the side chair across from Bry. Aster placed the cornbread, chicken, and soybeans in front of them. It looked delicious to Ceres, but of little interest to the men.

Aster sat and held her hands out to either side. Then she lowered her head and prayed.

"Dear Lord. Thank you for this great and wonderful day, for Ceres's hard work, Bry's hard work and the provision you've given Cane and me with the farm. Please bless this food. Let it give us nourishment to our bodies, make us strong and healthy. As it comes from your green earth, Amen."

Ceres lifted her head to Bry's staring.

"Pass the bread."

Ceres was off-put by Bry's awkward behavior. She thought he was a creep. She thought he must be to spend so much time with Cane. His visual appearance lent itself to a farm boy, nothing menacing or threatening. He was taller than her, with longer, golden-colored hair, deep brown eyes and a five o'clock shadow. He wore overalls the first day they'd met and so she thought of him like Lenny in *Of Mice and Men*, but the next few days he was in a pair of battered blue jeans and a grey t-shirt which made him more attractive.

Aster had caught Ceres daydreaming and playing with her mother's golden ring and said, "I wouldn't. It'd make Cane mad," as if she knew what Ceres was thinking. Ceres wondered if talking to Bry was tampering with something that wasn't hers, but she didn't really want to start any kind of romance with the help. However idealistic it seemed, she would be there too long to have a failed relationship staring at her across the fields.

She had learned all of Aster's duties in a month as her aunt's health rapidly declined. Aster started to look like Ceres's mother in the days before her death. They had the same quivering jaw, the same thinning and greyed lips. She was bedridden within the next week, but that didn't stop Cane's nightly visits to her bedroom for, what Ceres assumed he called, her "womanly duties." Ceres had heard him stumble into her room and slam the door. She would imagine him ripping off her blanket and her tugging at her nightgown in resistance. Ceres would pull the blanket over her ears in protest to what she thought she could hear.

She was too horrified to cry.

If she had been at school and heard a friend or roommate succumb to such treatment in the dormitories, she would've called the cops or barged in with a baseball bat. But it was different when it was her own family and that's the way things were. She might've been afraid to go in and save Aster, or that Cane would turn his eyes towards her. Mostly, she thought that it was none of her business and she didn't know whether or not Aster was saying no or if she was alright. She thought that was the problem with consent; sometimes it hides itself as obligation and no one is to say except the person consenting.

Genesis 9:13

"I have set my rainbow in the clouds, and it will be the sign of the covenant between me and the earth."

The day Aster died, she called for Ceres to come in her room after Cane left for the fields.

She looked somehow better than the weeks before. "You look nice, Auntie." Ceres managed a smile as she sat at the foot of her bed. The room was bright and yellow. It was as if the entire room was painted with Aster's spirit. The wallpaper had little purple flowers ensconced in green vines that, in any other situation, Ceres would think was hideous. But today, it was lovely. It was like she had walked into Aster's very being. Her soul was the entire room and she was inside it.

"If I'm going to meet my maker, I'd like to look nice."

Ceres laughed a little but then became even sadder. "You have to go?" she said.

"Afraid I do, but I'm not afraid Little One. It's time I go home to Him. I do hope safely to arrive at home."

Ceres started to cry. The words Aster said sounded so familiar. She covered her face.

"Oh not yet, please. Don't cry until I'm gone. I can't bear to leave you alone and crying." Aster propped herself up with the rest of her strength.

"Don't strain yourself, Auntie," Ceres begged.

Aster paid no attention and sat up. "Don't be prone to wander, Ceres." The girl had no idea what she meant. She chalked it up to near death delusion. Aster picked up her Bible and flipped to the very back. She then lifted out a small burlap pouch and held it tightly in her hand. "This will be your food," she said as she placed it in Ceres's hands and grasped them tightly. She squeezed until Ceres thought her bones would break and when she looked back up at Aster's face, the pain was gone and so was she. Her thin lips had parted slightly, having let out their last sweet breath.

She placed Aster's hands back on her stomach, folded them over each other and didn't know what else to do. *What are you supposed to do when someone dies?* She left the room and breathed heavily in the hallway, but it was nothing like the reprieve she received from stepping outside. She walked down the wooden steps to the flower and herb garden that Aster was growing and started to pull out all of the new growth. She pulled, angrily, at all of the basil, rosemary, lavender and thyme, ripping each root out of the ground with the bottom of the sprout. It was not their fault they were being treated so poorly. Finally, she collected the last of the daffodils and sat on the top step of the porch. She sewed the roots together, braiding the stems in a circle and tying in a daffodil on the right hand side. Her fingers slipped over the dirt- covered roots.

When she went back inside the warmth had left Aster's room. It was how she expected it, not that the room had actually lost its heat. Somehow it was eerie walking back into the room where she had just been. It was no longer Aster, but a dead person and she felt incredibly alone. She creaked open the door with the woven crown in her hand. Aster's hands had fallen to the sides, palms out as if in prayer. Ceres, shaking, placed the wreath on Aster's head, half expecting her to open her eyes and scare the daylights out of her. But she wouldn't be so lucky, and Aster wouldn't be so mean.

Ceres stared at her for a while, not really knowing how to stand, or what to do. She pulled out the pouch that Aster had given her moments before and opened it. She rolled seven corn kernels into the palm of her hand. They were all different in color; purple, blue, orange, red, pink, green and yellow. She thought of having a rainbow in her hand. She thought of Aster's message and thought surely she wasn't supposed to eat these dried seeds. She thought of her mother. Then she thought of Cane.

She placed the kernels back in the pouch and crossed the hall to her room, placing the treasure in the drawer where she had placed the antique brush the very first night she arrived. She pulled the drawer out all the way and placed her aunt's last gift at the back before replacing it. She did not know why these seeds were so important to Aster; perhaps she had truly lost her mind in the last minutes of her life. Either way, they were kept in her Bible, a place that Cane would never look, so she knew that they must have been of great importance.

Ceres marched solemnly to where Cane was loading the seed in his row planter.

His shoulders dropped and he spit. "You finally decide to come to work? Not on the field you don't. You go back to the barn where you belong."

"Uncle Cane…" she started.

"You can't work on the fields. You're not good enough to work on the fields." He kept working.

"Aunt Aster," she continued.

"Died," he said pouring more seed. "Dead."

"She just died."

He dropped the bag. "I'll see for myself." He whistled for Bry and he came as if from nowhere.

Ceres stood as Cane was replaced almost exactly without a seam. Her eyes darted from Bry to Cane to Bry again.

"I'd go," Bry said, "you don't want him alone with that old woman," he didn't even look up. Ceres's thoughts of Cane had not been so sinister, but they turned.

"He wouldn't," she said and Bry looked surprised.

"Okay."

Ceres made her choice and turned towards the barn. She was angry Bry had such a low opinion of her uncle, though hers had not been much higher.

Ceres spread meal through her fingers for the chicken, feeling every last kernel scrape the flesh between her fingers. She was startled when a man's voice said, "Go finish her room. You've done for the day." Spit. Stumble. Spit again.

Ceres put her bucket down and passed him, reeking of fresh alcohol and he lurched into her as she passed.

"Get the death out," he hissed through his teeth.

She walked back to the house and into Aster's room but her aunt was gone. On the floor, her broken herb chain lay in pieces; her sheets ruffled and damp. The frames had been taken apart, and her Bible lay face open on the ground, with bent pages.

Ceres picked up a slip of paper that had floated to the floor in the mess. She opened it to find what she thought were Aster's favorite Bible verses. Her mother had given her a similar list as a child, so she folded it and put it in her back pocket.

Cane had crested in Aster's room and whisked her out. *Where?* Ceres walked back into the main room when she heard Cane's truck roar.

The truck bed was full and covered with a white sheet, and swerved as Cane hit the gas and the wheels lost traction on the dirt road.

Ceres was in time to see whatever it was under the sheet roll and hit the side of the bed before rolling to the middle again, now somewhat uncovered.

She didn't need to see Aster's arm fall out from under the sheet to know it was her, but did anyway.

She was disgusted. Annoyed. Hateful. Sad. And worst of all, she felt trapped. With no other options, she went back inside and filled a bucket with water and detergent.

Night fell and Cane was still nowhere to be seen. Ceres heard the creaking of the swinging door into the kitchen from her room and got up to close her bedroom door. When she did, she saw it was Bry, and not Cane that had come in.

"You okay?" he asked, in the most normal way since they had met.

Ceres responded "yes" without thinking then slid to the floor. Bry came to her quickly and caught her arm.

"You don't seem fine," he said.

She involuntarily pulled him down to her and they sat in the doorway together. Ceres banged the back of her head on the doorframe as her eyes rolled back into her head. Bry moved to sit cross-legged awkwardly, like his legs didn't bend that way. He thought for a moment. "He won't come home," he said and got back up, "let's go."

"Where?"

"Just go. Don't you wanna get out for a minute?"

"What if he comes home?"

"He's not. He'll stay in town. I'll show you where he is. We'll spy on him."

Ceres thought Bry was peculiar, but was willing to take the risk of being murdered on the highway to get out of the farmhouse. Now that Aster was dead, it seemed like her future was certain; she would become Cane's alone and there would no longer be a protective barrier between her and her uncle. There was no telling what kind of atrocities Cane would be willing to inflict upon his "guest," claiming that it would be necessary to earn her bed.

She crawled into the passenger side of Bry's blue truck. It was exceptionally clean. The cloth upholstery had been recently vacuumed, as if he had anticipated the passenger. A faint smell of cigarettes filled the cabin.

"You smoke?" she asked.

Bry shook his head. "It's my dad's truck. He lets me use it 'cause he doesn't need it. But he smokes in it anytime he calls for me to take him somewhere," he looked embarrassed as he put the car into gear.

"It's okay; I don't even have a car." She looked outside and thought how she didn't have anything. "Where we going?" the squeal of the car and bump of the road made her voice almost unintelligible.

"Vera's Bar." *Of course he would be at a bar.* "It's a whore house."

Ceres's eyes widened.

"Well I guess I'm not surprised," she said.

"Man's got needs." Bry realized what he had said and quickly added, "Cane thinks he got needs that have to be filled every night." It wasn't any better. "I'm not like that." It just kept getting more awkward for the pair as the lights from the farm dimmed in the distance and the only light left was the shine of the truck's headlights.

She kept thinking it, so she finally said, "Why are you so awkward?"

"I'm sorry. I don't ever talk to anyone except my dad, and he is worse than me. And, I guess, Cane, but you know how he talks. I had Erv for a while too, but all he ever wanted to talk about was books and philosophy and then he went to school."

"Where's your mom?"

"Left."

Ceres was the one who felt awkward now. "Sorry."

"Don't be. She went to the city and she calls every once and awhile. She went back to school and met some guy that she liked better than me and Dad. So she'll send cards and ask me to dinner every once in a while but I don't much like the guy so I just as well stay on the farm and help Cane. He's an ass but at least he's simple."

It was the most she had heard Bry's voice. It was the longest stretch of speech she'd heard and he'd done it in one long, continuous breath. Towards the end, his voice had started to shake like he was telling secrets and the upholstery was absorbing them.

"You don't like things that aren't simple?" she asked.

"I guess not. When it comes to hard, I'd rather find something easy," he hit his palm against his temple.

Ceres started to laugh, "You're funny because you're so awkward."

Bry went from horrified to relieved.

"I'm happy you think I'm awkward," he chuckled then started laughing maniacally. Ceres thought it was funny at first, but as they made a turn off the road towards the river, she thought she might have made a life or death mistake in making fun of him.

"Is this where town is?"

"By the river, yes, this is where town is. Cane is right, you aren't too street smart."

"Then why are we stopping?" Her discomfort grew.

Bry just sniggered a little and got out of the car.

This is the end, she thought. Only, she didn't really mind. She just hoped that he wouldn't stab her. She thought that stabbing must be the most uncomfortable way to be murdered. It probably would be a stabbing, too. That's what happens out in the middle of the country. Girls get taken out to the middle of nowhere and they are raped and stabbed. She had a plan if something like this were ever to happen. She would pretend that she was interested in whoever had captured her and she would go along with it until she was somehow in control. Then she would bash him over the head with the closest hard object and run him over with the car they rode in on. She had devised this plan after a string of girls had been taken from the city near her school and found in the country twenty miles away, raped and stabbed. They had caught the man that was doing it, so it wasn't Bry, but she thought he could be a copycat murderer or a psycho all the same.

Bry's face appeared again on the driver's side and he zipped up his pants and opened the door.

"Sorry lady, just had to drain the lizard."

She made a face. "Gross. Why didn't you just go at the house?"

"I like peeing outside. In the river. All men do. It's like a thing."

Ceres laughed to herself. Bry repeated, "It's like a thing," because he thought that had made her laugh. What she was actually laughing at was that she thought Bry was going to kill and dump her body. "I'm growin' on you," he said putting the car back in gear.

She shook her head. "Don't you think people drink from that river?" she asked. "What about animals? Isn't it gross that you're peeing in something that someone down the road is going to drink?"

"Where do you think it goes when you flush it down the toilet, Ceres? Do you think it magically disappears and disinfects itself?"

She'd never thought about it before and now she felt bad. "Well at least there is hope that mine isn't going to be ingested by someone. Yours is a sure thing."

"Whatever you say, lady. I come from the earth, can't be that bad."

Sure enough, Cane's truck was parked badly in front of Vera's Bar. All the windows of the establishment were frosted black with only the outside lining illuminated with light from the inside.

Ceres got out of the cab and quickly went to the bed of Cane's truck to inspect its contents.

Nothing.

There wasn't anything there. Not even a sheet. Not even a blade of the wreath she had put in Aster's hair. She put her hand up to her face, but she couldn't smell the herbs, only bleach. She'd half expected her body to be left in the bed of the truck, unbending, in the back while Cane went to the whore house and received his nightly compulsion. Part of her was happy Aster was no longer there, the other half wondered where he had stashed her. Her thoughts went to the same imagined image of Bry burying her own dead, stabbed body by the river, only it was Cane digging the hole and Aunt Aster's sheeted body covered in blood.

"You comin' in?" Bry asked.

Ceres was confused, "I can?"

"Ya, it's a whore house. They'll let anyone in. They'll probably think you want to work here though," he smiled.

Ceres looked down at her modest jeans and loose fitting t-shirt, "Because I'm so slutty."

"No because most of the girls around here wanna make some money to get the hell out of town and into the city."

Ceres felt bad about her choice of words. She had a problem with judging everyone and everything around her. She thought maybe she really wasn't that smart.

"Cane'll see me and get angry. I'm not supposed to be here."

"He's long gone now."

"His truck is right here. He hasn't gone anywhere."

"Come on," he said opening the crimson door to Vera's. Ceres expected a saloon with a balcony; men chasing ladies around who had feathers in their huge, curled hair, fishnet stockings, lacy bustiers and men with mustaches and cowboy hats. When she walked in, it was just like a bar she'd seen in the city. The fluorescent lights behind the bar read various beer logos and the barkeep was well kept and young. There were wooden booths lining the walls and buckets of peanuts on the tables whose shells were being thrown on the floor by the patrons and smashed into the floor by waitresses to polish the wood.

"Hey guys," he said with a smile. "Get you a drink?"

Ceres looked at Bry in question if she could. He nodded and she ordered.

"Small towns don't care about IDs, lady," Bry said.

The ladies in the bar were dressed exactly like Ceres, save for tighter jeans and lower cut t-shirts. "I thought you said this was a whore house," Ceres said as they sat on the vinyl stools at the bar.

"You callin' me a liar?" he laughed. "It is," Bry continued. "See those rooms back there?" He pointed down the red lit hallway past the bar. The doors looked green and they were all shut. "Your uncle is just piss-ass drunk, passed out on the bed with a lady whose hands are full of his cash, just watching TV and smokin' a cigarette, laughing because it was the easiest money she's made all night."

"How do you know that?"

"Mark," he said beckoning the bartender. Mark looked up from drying glasses at the other end of the bar.

"What's up, Bry?"

"Where's Cane?" he paused, "Mindy?"

Mark laughed. He was a thirty-something man with a long mustache that he had twirled in mustache oil to make striking dark curls against his cheeks. His hair looked violet in the lights. He looked like he belonged in a 70s porn movie; a look often imitated in the city. "Room 5. Mindy came out a minute ago to get some paper towels. Your boy passed out in his own vomit right after he paid for her services so she felt obliged to clean it up. Most expensive cleaning lady he's ever had."

Ceres suddenly felt defensive of him, "You know his wife just died right?"

"Oh Mark, this is Ceres. She's his niece."

Mark looked her up and down. "Need a job?"

Ceres got up from her chair. "I'm out of here."

Mark laughed. "Calm down, lady! It was a joke. You know, something that you laugh at? I can tell you are way too uptight to be a lady of the evening." His last words trailed off in a southern drawl.

"You don't know that," she replied.

"So you do want a job," he said pointing at her with an upward palm.

"Seriously Bry, I want to leave," she said tersely.

"I thought you wanted to get out for a minute. See what life was like off the farm?"

"I know what life is like off the farm, and this is not it." She pursed her lips and walked out, the door jingling behind her.

She waited for what seemed like an eternity on the curb. Her eyes followed the businesses along the street across from Vera's. Next to the string of diagonally parked cars was a steakhouse boasting locally reared meat on the windows. There was a barber next door to that that had been closed for hours and then the small town's law firm that specialized in "farm law." The establishments were all part of the same main building, but had different facades to make them look like they were part of an old town.

She thought about lying in the bed of Cane's truck to be where the last warm person she knew was, until she realized it was insanely disturbing. She finally heard the jingle of the door behind her and stared coldly at the street in front of her.

"You ready?" Bry said getting in the car.

Ceres contemplated starting the walk home, but she should have started twenty minutes ago. The likelihood of being killed increased with walking alone down the country murder road; if it wasn't a murderous psychopath, it would be a drunk driver. Then she thought she shouldn't get in the car without an apology. Then she realized this was exactly why she didn't want to talk to Bry in the first place, because she didn't want to feel like she had to play all of the stupid girl games she played so well at school.

As she got into the cab, she squinted her eyes at him and said, "You are an asshole," then slammed the door of the truck behind her.

Bry was surprised. "Well, leaving without paying would make me an asshole. And paying and not drinking my order would make me stupid. So I guess we'll agree to disagree."

Ceres thought that he was right, but she would never say it. He was an asshole, but he wasn't the kind that she didn't want anything to do with like Cane. He was sincere. He might have been awkward but that was hardly an irrevocable flaw. He thought about what he was doing before doing it. Perhaps that was why he made her so uncomfortable. She had just jumped into everything that she had ever done, poking her nose around in things that weren't her business, not truly considering the consequences until she was knee deep in trouble.

"Your drink wasn't good. You'd be happy you didn't drink it."

That made Ceres's thirst grow. "Can you stop somewhere? Like a liquor store? I'll just get some drinks and drink them on my own." She thought maybe if small town bars didn't care about IDs, small town liquor stores wouldn't either.

"Oh, you're one of those," he said lifting his eyes to the road and turning his blinker on.

Ceres rolled her eyes. "I don't know why you are antagonizing me, but I just want to get a few drinks and forget that this whole thing exists."

"Then I'm not going to stop," he said turning his blinker off.

"Are you serious? That is so annoying." She crossed her arms in front of her.

"You should drink to have fun, not to drown your sorrows."

"Like you have any idea."

"Like you've tried to talk about it," he snapped back.

"If I tell you, will you stop?" She meant stop at the store, but she also wanted him to stop asking.

Bry pulled into the last strip mall before the darkness began again. They pulled into the spot in front of the drycleaners, next to the County LQ. Ceres wondered why anyone would need a drycleaner around here.

The girl walked down the aisles looking for vodka. She walked quickly away from Bry, as she was sure that he would have some smartass comment about what she was drinking, what kind of vodka it was, how much she was spending. His two-cents were annoying to her and she fully intended to drop him at the door of the house and drink alone.

She collected everything and went to the counter where Bry was standing and paying for a bottle of cherry vodka and diet cola.

"You've got a good one paying for your drinks, baby girl," the lady said handing Bry his change before Ceres got a chance to pull out her wallet. The cashier was an old wrinkled woman with formulaic blue shadow and red lips. She probably wasn't as old as she looked, no one Ceres met was. She had a long and slender cigarette hanging from her lips and she puffed on it as she spoke. Her skin was desiccated; it looked like she had thousands of tiny little rivets on her face.

"Thanks," she said grabbing the bag.

"You didn't have to pay for my stuff," Ceres said, secretly relieved she wouldn't have to risk the embarrassment of not having enough cash on her.

"I could tell you were going to ditch me with your booze at the farmhouse and I figure if I paid for it you couldn't just leave me at the door," Bry said stone-faced. She waited for him to laugh and he didn't. She just shook her head. "Plus, you're not of age."

"You shouldn't drink that crud," Bry said from the next room, cracking open a beer.

Ceres filled her glass with ice, a decent shot of vodka and diet cola.

"What, the vodka or the diet soda?"

"Diet Cola. It's full of chemicals."

Ceres looked at the back of the bottle at the ingredients.

Seeing her skepticism, he said, "Just tell me all of the ingredients you can pronounce."

She couldn't, so she said, "Because beer is so much better."

"My buddy owns this brewery a state over," he said tapping the label of the mountains. "We went for a tour last year. He makes it all himself so I know exactly what I'm drinkin'."

"Aren't you just the paragon of health."

"I don't know anything about it, Ceres. I just don't want to drink junk."

"But you'll pee in the river."

"It came from my body so it can't be that bad," he repeated.

"Is that your criteria for everything?"

Bry sarcastically nodded and went to sit in Cane's recliner. "You shouldn't be drinking at all," he said.

"Says the man who bought it for me. Plus, I went to private school in the city. What do you think happened there?"

Bry didn't know anything about it. "So this ain't your first rodeo?" he asked. Ceres rolled her eyes at the saying. She opened drawers and cabinets to find a glass of multicolored straws and umbrellas. She placed a blue and white straw in her drink, a yellow umbrella in the side and bent the straw gingerly before taking a sip. It made her feel as if she was on vacation. The ceramic roosters on the stove reminded her of Portugal.

They sat in silence for a few minutes before it started to get uncomfortable. Cane's recliner was worn down and the leather was soft with overuse. Bry leaned all the way back and kicked out the footrest. He took turns looking at the television in the corner of the room, to the window looking out to road from town to the house. Ceres sat in the stationary sofa chair next to it and studied the patterns and colors of the roped circle carpet on the floor underneath them. She started in the middle of the carpet with black and followed the spiral around to the outside that was a deep blue. As she followed it she thought of following the yellow brick road.

Ceres suddenly felt unstable as she started to feel tipsy and Bry started to look drunk.

She stood up. "Another drink?" he said, "Where you going to this time? Mexico?"

Ceres didn't know what he meant. "You're staring off to nowhere with your girly drink so I think you're probably daydreamin' of some island oasis." Ceres's discomfort grew with Bry's intuition. It seemed like he was able to read her mind, which made her wonder if he had known she thought he was going to kill her on the way to town earlier.

"I've never been to Mexico. We only went on cultural vacations when I was younger." She realized how that sounded, "not that Mexico doesn't have culture. I mean..."

"Now you're sounding like me!" he blurted.

She laughed. "Maybe you're rubbing off on me."

"Yep, you're definitely catching stupid."

"You aren't stupid, just weird."

They laughed genuine laughter from the bottom of their stomachs. It felt good to laugh and to mean it. She thought maybe they could be friends. Maybe they could share secrets like brothers and maybe they could escape together. But she didn't know if Bry wanted to leave.

After a while, Ceres got up and went through the swinging doors in the kitchen to the formal sitting room. She walked over to the old lavender chair and sat in it, stroking the material down to a soft purple and then up again to a deeper color. Bry came in after her and sat in the opposite Victorian chair.

"These chairs are miserable," he said.

"I don't know if they were designed to be comfortable," she said. "When you have people come in and sit in your sitting room, you want them to leave eventually.

That's why you keep them in your sitting room and that's why these chairs are so uncomfortable."

"You made that up," he said honestly.

"Yes, but it makes sense." She got up and went over to the fireplace mantel, picking up a picture of her Granddad and Omice. "These are my grandparents," she said without turning around. She picked up the picture next to the one that she put back down, "and this is Aster and my mom."

"What happened to your parents?" he asked mildly.

Ceres took the picture and sat down with it. "She died. She just didn't wake up one morning. They said they didn't know why. They did a bunch of tests. My dad had a toxicology test done. She just died. They said 'natural causes.' And then a few months later my dad died. They did the same thing, ran a bunch of tests. It was a few weeks before I graduated high school. They never said why he died. Just said 'natural causes' again like it was the stock thing to say when they are tired of trying to figure out why someone died. For a while I was worried I was next."

"You're still here," Bry smiled softly. "I'm sorry, Ceres."

"That I'm still here or that my parents died?" she said looking at the picture and running her finger over the face of her mom. "I think they are happy together, somewhere." She looked back up at Bry, "I think my dad died because he missed my mom so much. He must have missed her a lot to die, though. I missed her so much; I can't imagine missing her any more than I did."

Ceres awoke in her bed, the morning sun peering through the blue curtains. She admired their doily pattern and scalloped edges before wondering how she got into her bed. She sat up abruptly and lifted the sheets to see that she was still wearing all the clothes she had been wearing the night before. She sighed in relief. Then she panicked again thinking that it was late and she should've been out in the barn already. She didn't care as much that Cane would be angry. She cared that the animals wouldn't be fed.

As she got up she noticed her shoes neatly laid by the foot of the bed, a glass of water and some aspirin on her nightstand.

She walked out to the living room and noticed that something was different. She couldn't put her finger on it, but she knew that Cane would know it and point it out immediately. Something had been changed, moved, touched.

Then, she heard a muffled mixture of men talking on the porch and stepped lightly to the window to hear.

"I'm goin' in for a few days. You're in charge." Pause. "She's no good, you'll have to carry her weight."

She heard Bry laugh and say, "Ya."

Ceres felt like she should show him what carrying her weight around the farmhouse would look like.

"I've to arrange some kind of burial for the old bag. It'd look bad if I didn't. Then I'll stay at a friend's in town. Don't come into town. Just stay here and keep her here too. Don't let her get any ideas."

"Isn't her head full of too many ideas already?" Bry said and they both laughed.

Cane left to his truck and Bry opened the door to the house. Ceres was sitting in the front room on the old Victorian chaise.

"I'm so lazy, Bry. Carry me around. There are too many ideas in my head for me to hold it up straight!" She feigned weakness.

Bry looked serious. "You don't understand," he said seriously.

"No I get it. Boys' club. You don't need to explain that to me."

"If I spoke against him, I'd lose my job."

"I get it," she said staring off. Then she realized, "It's the pictures!"

"What?" Bry asked back. "What pictures?"

"All of the pictures are gone from the mantle. Did you take them?" she accused. Bry shook his head. "Did *I* take them somewhere?" she questioned. He shook his head again.

"Cane was here early this morning, maybe he moved'em or somethin'." Her eyes darted around the room, looking to see where they could be stashed, but unsure if she should go poking around when Bry was there. She didn't know if he could be trusted after the comment he had made on the porch. Her eyes darted back to his and she got up quickly, "Gotta get to work."

She fed all of the animals and then sat in front of the cow pen. The cows weren't particularly nice. Some of them were actually pretty mean. They were very protective of the littler ones, which was probably natural, but they would stare and snort at her in a menacing way if she got too close to one. This particular cow was ready to have calves and that was why it was inside, away from the heat. Ceres chalked up her mean attitude to her obvious discomfort and maternal instinct. Her belly protruded from either side of her body. It looked like she just needed to be milked for a few days straight to mitigate the bulge.

In an unusual and uncharacteristic move, the cow, who was called Dally, came to the edge of the pen and laid down, which was more like falling, in her state. She turned her huge brown eyes towards Ceres, like a dog awaiting his daily rub. Dally's long eyelashes batted before her stomach started to pulse, and a noise came from her that she had never heard before.

She was having her calves. Ceres was so interested that she moved to the other side of the pen to get a better look. She had never witnessed anything like it and it was the perfect time to realize that there was some greater plan than living her life in the misery of Cane's grasp.

Dally opened and a silver shimmer of goo emerged from her. Head first, the calf, encased in a fluid sac, slipped from her mother with little obvious effort. Ceres thought that perhaps childbirth was less difficult for animals, and then she thought it was probably because humans liked to complain, or perhaps it was really a punishment that God had given women because Eve tempted Adam with the apple. Whatever the reason for Dally's smooth labor, Ceres was happy for it. She could imagine nothing worse than hearing the cow moan in pain and not be able to help.

The calf fell to the floor beside her and Dally got up easily next to her new baby. She shuffled slightly, kicked and fell to the floor of the barn a second time with her head facing away from Ceres. Again she started the birthing process, this time it moved faster and the calf's head seemed to shoot out of its mother. Another push and the shoulders peeked out. Then nothing. Quiet. Then came the screams.

They were like nothing that Ceres had ever heard. Dally was convulsing, pushing, her stomach was pulsing with pain. She had thrown her head back, contorting her spine into a position that looked as if she had snapped her own neck. Her mouth open and gurgling.

Ceres ran. She ran out of the barn into the sunlight; each ray piercing her retina that had been encased in shadow after hours of hiding from her own reality in the barn. She was shouting as she pumped her arms to try to run faster. She was an animal, sprinting for her life, only it wasn't her life that she was worried for.

When she reached Bry she collapsed and barely muttered that he needed to go to the barn.

"What are you tryin' to say?" he asked.

"Jus' go to the...barn. Dally's...Dally's..."

"Having her calves and you couldn't handle it?"

"The calf's stuck."

And Bry ran too.

She arrived moments after Bry hopped the gate and started pulling on the calf's shoulders. He turned her and pulled her to the now haunting sound of Dally's cries.

"What is happening?" Ceres breathed heavily, trying to regain herself.

"She's stuck," he said. He was calm. He was straining but he was oddly and obviously calm.

Ceres watched as he shifted the calf and himself into various positions, trying to pull out the young animal delicately. He was a stark contrast to how she had left the scene to come get him. He was calm and composed; she had been frayed and unsure. When she was running from the scene it was bloody and gruesome in her mind. With Bry in the barn it was beautiful again.

Bry slipped the second calf from Dally as she collapsed her head onto the straw, much like Ceres had expected.

"I'd get out but she's too tired to get me," Bry laughed, but something was wrong.

"Why isn't that one moving?" Ceres asked.

The second calf lay motionless on the ground, eyes open. The only sound in the barn was the severe huffing of Dally's deep breaths. Bry had to kneel down to see if the calf was breathing. He ran his hand over her stomach and said, "Didn't make it," disappointed.

Again, Ceres was faced with a death in the room with no idea how to act.

"What do we do?" she asked. "Do we take it out? Why did she die? Is Dally going to die?"

"You sound like you're five years old with all those questions," he said.

"Do you think she suffocated? Do you think she'll come back? Can you do something? Bry, do something," Ceres said frantically.

Bry was visibly upset. "Listen!" he yelled, "I can't do nothin'! Can't you see that I tried to save her? Didn't work. Stop askin' questions that you already know the answer to. I can't do nothin' else."

Bry passed her and she reached out for his arm but he shrugged it away.

"Finish your jobs, I'll finish this," he said callously. She thought he sounded like Cane. He collected a towel and went back over to the calf. Ceres just stood motionless. She couldn't decide if she couldn't move or that she wouldn't.

Bry took the towel and threw it over the calf then picked her up and lifted her out of the pen and into the wheelbarrow. He threw the towel on the floor of the barn and Ceres went to collect it. Ceres looked at the calf in the wheelbarrow. There was something strange about it. She wasn't just dead; she was contorted, like she had been tortured in her own mother's womb.

"Bry, I'm not going to ask you any more questions. This is more of a statement," she said. "That doesn't look like a healthy calf."

"It's not healthy; it's dead," he said half-jokingly.

"Look there," she said pointing at the calf's stomach and hind legs, "that's not normal for a calf, right?"

Bry inspected the bulging stomach and again ran his hand over what looked like a large tumor in the belly of the calf. He pushed it lightly at first, then harder. The calf hawed and, as if possessed, spewed blood and sputum out of her mouth, filling the wheelbarrow with blood.

"Is she alive?" Ceres said, horrified.

"No. It's a death cough," he said taking out his knife and slitting the calf's throat.

Ceres gasped, "If she was dead, why did you do that?"

"Make sure." Bry could see her unease. "Listen, she couldn't have survived twenty minutes anyways with that lump and those jacked up legs."

"Why are you so nonchalant about it? Don't you think that it's weird that the little one is so deformed?"

Bry shook his head, "We see this a lot on the farm. Lately."

That night, Ceres made macaroni and cheese from a box and opened up a can of meat to cut up into it. Her mother had made it for her when she was little, and she needed to feel her somehow. When she shook the upside down can onto a plate, it slid out with a thick layer of gunk from the can surrounding it. She couldn't help but think of the meat— of the cow that had been killed in the barn. She looked at the can and thought that it was not *real* meat. She turned to the trash and threw it away.

When Bry came into the kitchen she was surprised. She didn't know what to say. There was too much that she had seen that day for her to say anything about anything else, and she knew that he wouldn't want to talk about it.

Bry looked down into the trash can. "Why did you throw that? It's perfectly good meat," he said taking a fork and getting it out.

"You can't eat that," she said.

"It's just a little trash; I'll just wash it off."

"Well there's that, but it's gross. I won't eat it. It's gross that meat can look like that."

"Ceres, you have to eat." Bry sat at the table.

"I don't have to eat that," she said uncomfortably. "How come this meat's ok and my soda wasn't?" She challenged him but didn't wait for an answer. "Don't you ever eat at home?" she said.

"No, it's part of how Cane pays me. I don't have to eat with my dad. I'll leave after I eat. And some things are more obvious than others. That drink blatantly said it was gonna be bad for you on the side of it."

"You don't have to leave. I just wondered." Ceres dished him some macaroni and slimy meat. "Plus, I need a legal guardian," she said sarcastically.

They sat in silence for a minute then Ceres clasped her hands together and tried to remember Aunt Aster's prayer, "Dear Lord." She muttered, "Thank you for this great and beautiful day, for hard work, for Bry's hard work and my hard work... bless this food, please. Let it nourish us and make us strong. Amen."

"As it comes from your green earth, Amen," Bry said before opening his eyes.

Ceres sat on the porch of the house after dinner. She sipped on a beer that she had found in the back of the refrigerator. The sun was setting over the farm and it was beautiful. The sky chose shades of pink and violet on top of the orange hue left over by the falling sun. She appreciated it today.

"What you gonna do with those seeds?" Bry said.

Ceres kept looking forward. "What seeds?" she felt goose bumps at his assertion.

"You told me about them. Then you said '*shh, it's a secret*'"

Ceres was embarrassed. "I don't know. I don't know how to even plant them."

"Take one and put it in the soil over there," he said pointing at the seeded corn field. "See if it grows."

"How will I know which corn husk it produces if I plant it with the rest of the corn?" she asked.

"Shoot, that's right." He thought for a minute, "Plant it right at the edge, that way it will get the water and the spray. We'll put a flag in the ground where it's planted so we'll know which one it is when it comes up."

Ceres thought for a while and then figured Aster would've wanted her to try. "I'm just going to do one. If it doesn't grow, I want to save the rest of them to remember her."

Ceres went inside and told Bry to stay out on the porch. She didn't want to share her hiding place with him. She went into her room, closed the curtains and shut the door, like she was in some seedy motel. She pulled out the drawer of her night stand and pulled out the pack of seeds. She dumped them into the palm of her hand. She picked the blue one, though she didn't know why. Maybe because the blue one looked like it could reach the heavens.

When she came back out, Bry had a cardboard pot in his hands.

"That's a good idea," she said.

"It's for your seed. We're going to put in into this biodegradable pot and have it stick out of the soil a quarter inch. That way it'll still get the water and spray and we don't have to put a flag up that'll catch his attention if he ever comes back," he said as if she needed it to be explained further.

"Is there a chance that he won't? I mean, is there a legitimate possibility that he just will never come back from town?" Ceres showed her distain.

Bry shook his head. "Probably not. He'll stay in town for a week at the most. He's never trusted me with the farm longer than that. He'll probably be back sooner than later cause he don't trust you at all."

Ceres thought that he shouldn't, but she wasn't sure why.

It was dark, so they had to take dirt from the herb garden for the planter. Ceres thought that it would help make the seed grow because the garden was Aster's and the seeds were familiar with her. When they had sowed the seed in the pot, Bry lit a lantern and they walked out to the cornfield.

Ceres started to feel unsafe again. "Why the lantern? Don't you have a flashlight?"

"Yeah but this is more fitting."

"Why is that?"

"We're going out and doin' something we shouldn't be doin'. Flashlights are for police, not for criminals. Lanterns are for fugitives."

Ceres liked the idea of being a fugitive and her feelings of unease lessened. They went to the edge of the field and Bry cut the soil with his shovel. The sound of it was unmistakable. She had heard it in her head when they had stopped by the river. Unease returned.

Ceres knelt on the soil with the pot in both of her hands as Bry waited. She stared at the hole in the ground.

"Did they bury her?"

"Aster? Probably. They don't let dead be unburied for long."

"Why wouldn't they have a funeral?"

"She didn't get respect when she was alive. What makes you think he would let anyone, let alone him, pay her any last respects when she was dead?"

"I would have," Ceres said at the ground.

"I would have, too," he paused, "Put it in the dirt Ceres and let's get back."

Ceres put it in the hole, leaving a small round rim of brown above the soil. It was as if the pot was drowning. She imagined it a person, only his head, cocked all the way back in the ocean. Bobbing with the waves. As the dirt filled the outsides and some of it fell into the pot, she imagined being choked by the ocean water.

"What if it grows an' grows an' grows to the clouds?" he asked.

"Then we'll climb it," she replied.

Cane didn't come back for a few days. In the meantime, Bry would sleep on the couch. He felt like her protector. He mainly didn't want her to be alone when Cane came raging through the door, drunk as hell and not a care for the fact that she was his niece. He could tell that it would probably be the end of his employment at the farm. There was a ticking time bomb in the room and it was only a matter of time before Bry would have to make the definitive move to save her instead of himself.

When Cane did come in, it was morning. He wasn't drunk, or mad. He seemed relaxed and rejuvenated. He hit the recliner that Bry had fallen asleep in the night before with a laugh, "Get up you lazy son-ova-bitch!"

Bry startled. As he started an apology, Cane said, "Great job on the farm. Really great job. Just did rounds an' everything looks great." Bry didn't know what was going on. "I'm sure Ceres was helpful too, right?"

"That seems sincere," he said skeptically.

"Ya, she ain't so bad," Cane replied.

"You okay?" he asked.

"Why? I'm great! The old hag is gone, the farm looks like it's gonna have a great year. I've got you in my employment and did I mention the old hag?"

Ceres didn't know Cane was back until she went out to feed the animals and his truck was outside. She had goose bumps develop on her arms so she pulled down her sleeves and walked a little faster to the barn.

When she walked into the barn, there he was. Standing over by Dally and her calf.

"Only one," he said as she walked in.

"There were two," she murmured.

"Died on the way out, I hear."

"Yes," she hesitated, "and it was deformed."

"Deformed how?" he asked.

"It had a huge tumor in its belly and its legs were really small."

"How small?" he said, walking towards her.

"I don't know, a few inches?" she stepped back.

He stopped right in front of her and took her hand. He pushed up her sleeve and ran his calloused fingers up the inside of her arm. "Show me where the leg stopped" his voice slithered towards her.

She jerked her arm away quickly and picked up her bucket of feed from the wall. "It was exactly six inches. They were exactly six inches long."

She knew that her days without conflict were limited.

That night, Ceres lay in her bed staring at the ceiling. She had heard Cane stumble up the stairs a half hour before, hitting the walls and dragging his feet as he went along. She couldn't sleep. She kept thinking about Dally, the calves. She thought about her mother and father and longed for someone to comfort her before convincing herself that she was old enough not to have to be comforted. She thought about the pictures on the mantel of the fireplace in the front room. *Where were they?* She got up and placed her feet on the cold wooden floor.

As she opened her door, she felt the cold air from the hallway hit her face. She thought that she should turn around. She didn't know how Cane would react if he found her snooping around late at night. She didn't know, but she thought that surely he wouldn't like it. Aster knew how he would react. Aster would have protected her.

Her feet padded softly down the hallway until her weight creaked the wood floor underneath her. She winced a little and clenched her fists before moving towards the front room.

When she made it there, her eyes had adjusted to the darkness. The fireplace in the front room was glowing with embers. The popping of the burned wood was the only sound in the room. She crouched down to the magazine holder next to the fireplace pokers and tongs. She flipped through the magazines, but could see there were no pictures hiding in the metal holder.

She got up and moved across the floor to look under one of the chairs when she heard the sound of springs hawing and several loud thumps clamoring across the floor above her. She looked towards the hallway, but there wasn't any time.

Cane was down the stairs in a hurry. Ceres tried to make herself as small as possible behind one of the Victorian chairs. He swayed back and forth as he tumbled down the stairs and to the front door, making sure that he had locked it. He turned around and glared through the room. Ceres had her back to him. She turned her face towards the fireplace. She thought she could reach the poker quickly if he attacked her or tried to punish her for being out of her room.

He moved slowly. Coughed. Scratched himself. She held herself on her haunches until her quadriceps started to burn. She finally heard him move back towards the stairs. She saw him look towards the hallway for a minute before retreating.

She fell forwards towards her knees and looked straight ahead. There, in the waste bin were the silver and gold framed images of her family. She took them out of the trash and hid them with the seeds.

As if he could sense the tension, Bry asked to move into Aster's old room. Cane had a problem with it at first, but Bry sold it like he would be available for work whenever Cane wanted and that he would keep an eye on Ceres so she didn't pull any funny business.

After he got used to the idea, he pretended like it was his own in a classic Cane manner.

Things went seamlessly for weeks. Ceres kept to the animals and made meals for the threesome. She didn't have any more strange encounters with her uncle. She stayed in her room and didn't go poking around in places she shouldn't. She thought that there was probably a good reason Aster told her to keep to herself. Bry helped Cane with the fields and Cane didn't drink. He eyed Ceres every once in a while, but every time he did, it seemed that he went into town for the night. Ceres enjoyed it most when he was gone. She and Bry would sit on the porch after dinner and tell stories about Aster and Erving. They would go and check in on their burgeoning corn plant and joke about what kind of giants they were going to find in the sky.

Bry had grown on her, but every once and awhile he would say something stupid that reminded her that it wasn't okay to date him. She would never date someone with "such an inferior intellect" she thought. Once she thought it, she realized what a horrible person she was and she'd be nicer to him the next day, or at least until he said something foolish again.

*

The day the Foundation came to visit, Ceres was late out of the house. She hurriedly opened the door to a young woman in a side ponytail and a tall and slender man, both in blue jeans and cowboy hats. She did not know where they were coming from, or what they wanted, but they looked like they belonged there, which made her feel more comfortable with strangers at the door.

"Hello little lady," the man said in a low voice, "man of the house home?"

Ceres looked at the young woman, who smiled a demure smile, and then back at the tall man.

"May I ask who is calling?" she said.

The man took off his hat and placed it over his heart, as if he was promising, "Mort Darbinger, little lady. Sorry for the rude greeting. Just wondering if the man of the farm is havin' trouble with this little big guy we call Abaddon?" He signaled the young girl to open a wooden box with a glass viewer to show Ceres the creature. Ceres went up on her tip toes and craned her neck to see nothing at first and then the fanned tail of a glorified caterpillar.

"Looks pretty harmless to me," Ceres scoffed.

He sneered, "Man of the house please." No more "little lady," no little smile.

"One moment please," Ceres taunted and shut the door.

Cane and Bry were out at the back of the house, fixing the leaky roof, so she wouldn't have to go very far.

"Uncle Cane, you have some visitors from somewhere with a caterpillar in a box."

Cane climbed quickly down the ladder and handed Bry the hammer. "You finish," he said and wiped his hands on his jeans.

"Apparently he's familiar with the bug," she laughed to Bry.

"Well, Ceres, you would be too if you were paying any attention on the field." He hammered.

Ceres shook her head, "What is it? And I haven't seen them. I'm not *allowed* on the field."

Bry climbed up the ladder. "They're not easy to see, but they eat a hole in the stalk and then they climb their way up to the corn and they ruin your entire harvest."

"Oh," she said.

"Those people are probably selling us some new spray," he said with his last blow to the roof.

"Pesticide?" she asked.

"Yep. This stuff isn't working as well as it did last season so I bet they are here trying to get us to spend more money to get rid of the pest. So ya, pesticide."

Bry could see the concerned look on her face. "You have to eat, Ceres. And in order for you to eat, you have to grow food, and if these bugs are comin' up and killing your food, eventually you're gonna die of hunger."

Ceres slid through the screen door to hear the conversation in the dining room. She hid behind the wall, by the stairs leading to the cellar.

"What you gonna do, Cane? Let your crop die and lose money or lose money now?" Mort pounded his fists on the table and the young lady cupped her hand over his to soften the sound.

He tempered his voice only slightly, "Just think of it as an investment, Mr. Cane. If you don't take care of the Abaddon now, it will just come back to your fields next year because it'll know that you aren't going to do nothing about it. And it will tell its friends. And it will lay its eggs. You don't really have a choice."

"No, no, Baby, he has a choice. He just gotta make the right one," the lady said sweetly.

There was quiet in the room. Ceres peeked her head from around the corner to see the wooden box being spun around on the table. Sweat was pouring down Cane's brow and the young girl smiled, tapping her cowboy booted heel on the floor.

Cane panicked, "Show me the stats again."

The man breathed heavily and pulled them out of his coat pocket. He laid them on the table and sighed. "Cane, you can see these but you know the bottom line."

Cane looked up at him. There was something in her uncle's eyes that Ceres had never seen before.

"We'll own your farm. We own you. If you don't do well this year an' pay your dues, the last due you pay will be with this house," Mort lifted his palms up to the ceiling. It reminded Cane of Aster, praying to God that they would have sustenance, that they would survive another year, and that they would live in this house *until the day they died.* "Our records show we've been doin' business with this farm for 40 years. That's a long account. Goes back to the days when Mr. Dierts himself would go door to door with seeds and spray. All to help farmers. I wouldn't want to break tradition. Would you?"

Compelled, Cane grabbed the pen off of the table and signed the dotted line on the top of the stack of paper. The young lady squealed with happiness and the slender man grinned so wide that he revealed the shiny gums of his teeth.

The blue drums were unloaded on the outside of the farm and the couple drove off in their oversized truck. Presumably they were going to the next farm to hawk their next shipment of fear and coercion in the guise of *tradition.* Cane told Bry that he was going to town and that he wasn't to touch the delivery until he got back. He said that "Adagmen will wait until we get to him tomorrow, son-ova-bitch."

Matthew 19:23-24

"Then Jesus said to his disciples, 'Truly I tell you, it is hard for someone who is rich to enter the kingdom of heaven. Again I tell you, it is easier for a camel to go through the eye of a needle than for someone who is rich to enter the kingdom of God."

Ceres fed Dally and the chickens. She patted Dally's calf, Betsy, on the head and rubbed the skin in between her eyes and down her nose. Then she headed back to the farmhouse to start lunch.

The dark blue drums were all lined up next to the light blue of the house. They were shining in the light and blinding to look at directly.

Ceres walked towards them and sat down in front of them. They were still a few yards away; she felt she should keep a distance.

She sat and looked at the tons of liquid that were encased in the buckets.

She squinted her eyes as she saw a black skull and cross-bones on the white label. She couldn't make out the wording so she inched closer and closer until she could finally read:

> **This product is toxic to fish and small mammals. This product may cause severe allergic reactions such as anaphylaxis. Do not apply to water or areas where surface water is present. Do not drink water that could be contaminated as it is highly poisonous to humans and animals.**

Do not apply this product or allow it to drift into blooming crops or weeds where animals or insects such as bees may be present. Highly flammable. Do not ingest. This product will kill you rapidly.

Ceres stood up and walked inside. *This product will kill you rapidly.*

She passed the fireplace where the pictures of Aster and Cane used to be on the mantle. *This product will kill you rapidly.*

Suddenly, she thought about Aster's death, and snap peas. She thought of a tradition of 40 years on the farm.

Ceres sat on the floor with her back against the bed and her eyes out the window. She picked the burgeoning hole in the knee of her jeans. She stretched her feet out to the vent in the wall under the window and arched her back to lie her head on the bed. She thought about her father. She thought about how they used to go on long walks and he would tell her that she would do great things. This didn't seem like a great thing. This was death to her. She was surrounded by death. All she knew was death. She saw Aster's face, jaw open and lifeless; Dally's calf, neck slashed and blood filling the wheelbarrow; the stark black face of a skull and crossbones on a dozen blue bins; her dad, in failing health, making his way up the path to her; her mother's sweet face.

Bry came to the doorway. She could hear his boots clunk down the hall.

He stopped and leaned on the doorframe.

"You're ok?" he asked.

She gasped for air as if she had forgotten to breathe. It was unexpected and she fell forward in shock, hugging her knees. Silence.

"Ceres, you okay?" he repeated.

"Yes," she said into her hands.

She felt him move towards her and she felt the air push up into her palms from the weight of his body sitting on the floor next to her.

"You hate it here," he said.

She laughed into her hands, "It's been weeks and it doesn't get any better. You know, I thought that the death was done. Everyone, I mean everyone, has died."

Bry put his hand on her knee and picked at her jeans where she had been picking moments before. "Death is part of life. You have to live in order to die. You have to die in order to live."

Ceres lifted her head to him, "I don't want to have to die here."

He moved and sat cross-legged next to her, "You will not die here."

"But do I have to live here?"

"Are you really living here now?"

Ceres believed that her body was there, but she didn't know about anything else. She put her hand over Bry's and intertwined her fingers with his. She knew that her purpose was bigger than this farm.

The back door slammed in the middle of the night while Ceres and Bry were asleep soundly in their beds. Cane stumbled softly, hitting the recliner and bouncing back to the wall, then through the kitchen, swinging through the wooden doors to the hallway. He belched, drunk, then kicked off his shoes at the bottom of the stairs. He looked at the six stairs to the next landing in front of him and decided they were too much. He looked down the hall and then back at the stairs. He placed his foot on the step and then pivoted decidedly down the hallway. His eyes half shut. His mouth open.

He whipped off his over shirt to reveal his dirty pig's skin and threadbare wife beater. His body dragged behind his mind, like he was walking through sludge or mud. Without even thinking twice, he slid into Ceres's room.

She didn't move when the light from the hallway grew and waned over her face. Cane closed one eye to focus on the image, but couldn't quite make anything out but shapes. He pulled his jeans all the way down to the floor and kicked his feet out of them, leaving them in a pile. His socks were loose and discolored on his feet. He lifted up the cover and slid in between the sheets. As he got closer, his vision wasn't any clearer and he made his mind to just look through half-closed eyes. He laid down next to her, bouncing the bed with his added weight. The springs made a noise beneath them. He moved his cold and dirty hand over her stomach, moving his hand down to her bare skin and then up underneath her shirt. She didn't wake, but her eyelashes fluttered and she turned onto her side, facing away from him. He pulled her back onto her back.

"No," she whispered. "Not now." And she moved back over to her side. She thought that it was Bry, misreading her earlier actions as an invitation. As soon as she moved away from Cane, she was abruptly and forcefully pushed back onto her back. She opened her eyes startled, as Cane slammed his hand over her mouth. She could smell the liquor seep from his skin; his body odor flared the hair in her nostrils. She thrashed her head to the side and his hand followed it.

"No dear, now's fine," he said shifting his body under the sheets.

Ceres was in terror as she tried to get up and he pushed her deeper and deeper into her bed. She felt as if the bed was going to swallow her, that she would be swathed into the mattress and into the floorboards. She was being buried alive.

"You don't scream. You'll only wake'em and he's got a long day at work tomorrow," Cane murmured. His words strung together as if they were continuous.

His weight pushed all of the air out of her ribcage. She was crushed. He was crushing. She wondered why she was not able to overpower him, though it was not for lack of trying. He was not a big man; he was small, slender, but as she struggled she felt his muscle, hard over her, pushing her in violence. She didn't ever want to touch him in this way. She had never wanted to touch him at all. His skin was rough and grainy; his smell thick and nauseating. She remembered wondering what it was like for Aster to be with such a horrible man and she regretted that thought, thinking that maybe she had willed the answer.

He was holding her arm with one hand, his forearm and elbow shoved in her mouth. Her lips were pressed against her teeth, thinning her skin uncomfortably until she opened her mouth from the pressure. Her other arm was immovable under his weight. He pulled down her pajamas. Ceres's jaw was strained by the jabbing movement of the elbow in her mouth. She tried to bite him, but her jaw was unable to hinge. His grip tightened on her arm. She stared at the ceiling. She squeezed her eyes shut and prayed. She wished that she would have taken a baseball bat to him when she had heard the noises from Aster's room before. She tried to flop her stomach to gain some leeway but was unsuccessful.

She thought this was it. He wouldn't kill her, *but she wouldn't live past this.*

Suddenly he stopped and fell limp on her body. She thrashed her head and wiggled his elbow out of her mouth and turned her head to see Bry standing over them.

"Help!" she whispered. "I can't." And her mind fell into the shadows of the room, her eyes into the back of her head.

Both Cane and Ceres had blacked out on the bed, only she willingly. Bry pulled Cane from her body from under the man's arms. He dropped Cane on the floor when he saw her body, naked below the waist. He quickly pulled up her pants and carried her to his bed. He covered her with his blankets and pulled Cane upstairs.

Ceres awoke in the bed that Aster died in. She stared at the yellow wallpaper with purple flowers. She remembered Aster. The white and yellow striped curtains intensified the yellow light from the sun in the room. Bry was asleep in the wooden chair next to her, a shotgun in his lap.

She put her hand on his knee and shook it. He opened his eyes, "You're ok."

She sat up in the bed, "I can't remember." She pulled the striped yellow comforter up under her chin and crossed her legs.

"It's better that way."

"Why do you have the shotgun?"

Bry looked at her in a telling way. She knew that he was afraid that Cane would've come back.

"Thank you," she said.

"I knew it would only be a matter of time. I just thought he would've stayed in town. I was caught off-guard."

"Me too," she said admiring the new bruises on her arm.

They stayed in the room until they heard Cane come down the hallway and knock on Bry's door.

"Kid, you up? Let's go. We've gotta spray today."

"I'll be a minute."

"Okay." And they heard him clunk down the hall again.

"I guess he doesn't remember me punching him in the back of the head last night," Bry laughed.

"So it won't be awkward when I see him today, you think? He won't remember what he did last night?" Ceres asked.

"Probably not. I'll talk to him today and see."

"Too bad I won't forget it."

"I thought you said you didn't remember."

Bry met Cane by the buckets and loaded them into the back of Cane's truck. They were silent mostly, avoiding every chance to talk about what a horrible person Cane was and how Bry had protected Ceres from him. That was until Cane said, "I should'a stayed in town last night."

Bry kept working.

"Why d'you say that, Cane?"

"Don't remember drivin' home. Don't remember gettin' in a fight. Don't remember much but I took off my pants somewhere and I can't find'em," he laughed. "I'ma damn good drunk driver, son!" he laughed again.

"If you're good at it, you should keep doin' it," he replied with a smile.

"Damn straight. I might just do it tonight. Save me some money from stayin' in town."

Bry wished he would stay in town forever. He wished he could make Cane disappear, not just for Ceres, but for himself too. He wished that he could take over the farm. He wished that he was Cane's son so he would inherit the land. No one would inherit the farm, though. With all of his debts, it would go to the Foundation. He wished his own father would have been either less of a drunk or more of one. He wished the same of Cane.

They got into the cab of the truck and went to spray the corn fields.

When Bry and Cane returned for dinner, they both ran in from outside and into the bathroom to wash off. In reality, they should've been wearing suits, but they figured long sleeves were enough. Bry pulled all of his clothes off and piled them on the bathroom floor before getting into the ice cold shower and hopping around and shaking with the chill.

Ceres only saw the panic from the kitchen. She was sick of being there. She liked cooking, but all she ever had to work with was frozen corn, or soy beans, or a chicken that she had cared for desperately, dead and plunked in a glass bowl for her to clean out and bake. She hated the smell of the food freezers in the cellar. They smelled like old ice and old food. She didn't want to eat any of it anymore.

At dinner, when Cane and Bry came to the table, Ceres intentionally made the food as disgusting as possible. She thought that either Cane would hate it so much he wouldn't make her cook anymore, or he'd give her something else to work with.

Cane chewed the food slowly; Ceres expected him to spit it down the table at her. "Not your best, girl," he said. "You feelin' sick?"

Ceres picked at the overcooked and under-seasoned chicken on her plate. "It'd be better if I could get some spices, maybe some groceries?"

"When you live on a farm, you make your own groceries," he replied choking down another bite.

Ceres looked at her plate, disheartened, when a wad of cash landed on her soy mash.

She looked at Cane in question, "So I can go?"

"Bry'll drive you in. Don't waste my money. Keep my receipt. Don't buy any dairy, corn, soy, chicken or beef. Don't waste my money, girl. There is nothing I hate more than wasted money."

He threw his card at Bry, "Fill the truck."

It wasn't dark when Bry and Ceres headed into town. The sun was just starting to set, creating a pink hue to the sky.

The pair bumped up and down in the cab of the car. Bry had a blue cap on that shaded his eyes from Ceres's view.

"I packed my things today," she said looking down the road.

"Why?" he looked over.

"I can't be there anymore. I'm going to leave."

"Right now? When are you leaving?"

"I don't know. I want to look around in town to see where I can get with the money I have. I'll be eighteen in a few months. It won't matter that I'm leaving then"

"Why did you tell me that? What am I supposed to do with that information?"

She shrugged. She didn't know what she wanted him to do with the information. She didn't know why she told him.

"Forget it."

Bry took his hat off and messed his hair, "No, Ceres, I'm not gonna forget it. Where the hell are you going to go?"

Ceres was shocked at his choice of words, "You want me to stay? You want me to risk *every* night? You want me to just lie in my bed waiting for my uncle, *my uncle*, to come into my room and attack me? Whatever, Bry, I thought you would understand. This is ridiculous."

Bry threw his hat on her lap. He thought about telling her that he would protect her, that that was why he moved into the farmhouse in the first place. Instead he said nothing.

"You could come," she said softly.

"I can't. It's my job."

Ceres remembered what her dad always said so she repeated it for him, "You shouldn't live for your job."

Bry laughed, "I'm living for myself. My future. My family."

"Well I have to create all of those things. Cane's all the family I have left, so I guess I don't have that to live for. I can't have a future here. There's nothing for me here."

"That's nice, Cer."

"I told you to come with me."

"And I can't."

They pulled up to the fueling station and Bry couldn't get out of the car fast enough. He opened the cap on the side of the car and filled the tank with 99% premium corn-fuel. Bry figured that he had Cane's card, so he might as well put in the good stuff.

Ceres leaned her head in her palm and rested her elbow on the window. They were the only car in the station. The lights were as bright as daylight and everything looked clean and silver with accents of red on the pumps. There were no straight lines on the whole station. Everything was contoured, as if it anticipated the high winds over the nearby fields.

At the store, Ceres walked the aisles alone. She held her basket like it was supposed to carry flowers. She walked slowly; she was trying to irritate Bry, who hadn't spoken since rejecting her plan to abscond from the farm.

Ceres's eyes skimmed over the products that she used to buy with her allowance. She looked at the silly meals that she bought in bulk for the student dorms, the packages were shining with fluorescent lights. She laughed thinking about her senior year when all she ate were ramen noodles when studying for her economics tests.

She picked up three or four of the noodle packets and placed them in the basket. She would keep them for later. She picked out some garlic and onions, some carrots and black pepper. She ran her hands over the apples before she placed three in the basket.

She waited by the produce until the showers came on and she put her hand in the water, letting the water splash off of her hand and into her face. She closed her eyes and thought of pickle jars and her mother's apple pies. Aster had made the same kind the week before she passed away. Ceres thought about how long ago it seemed that she had felt love, the kind of love that radiated through a person and she missed it.

She made her way back to the front when she saw Bry resting on the brown and yellow mechanical horse at the front of the store. He leaned against the horse's side and crossed his legs in front of him. She felt, now, that she could feel love from him.

She passed a stand next to the produce that read "All you'll ever need!" with shelves of white bottles underneath. A video embedded inside the display was tripped by Ceres's presence. It was a young and attractive man who spoke in a smooth and convincing manner:

Are you sick of being sick? Are you sick of all the chemicals making their way into your foods? Into your water? Us too! These pills are all you'll ever need! Each pill has the right servings of carbohydrates, fiber, sugar, fats, nutrients and vitamins. How do they work you ask? Well I'm glad you want to know! The pill is the size of a grain of rice. You take it with a full glass of regular water. The pill makes its way down to your stomach where it expands to the size of a full size meal, this way you'll feel full. Then, it releases all of the nutrients you need into your bloodstream. Sound alright? It sure does! After four hours, the pill deflates and makes its way to your bowels where it is disposed of. You'll never have to eat again! Your calories will be met with the ease of taking a pill. And guess what? We are certified natural and good for your bones, eyes, heart and health. Try a bottle today! It's all you'll ever need!

She picked up the bottle and Bry moved off his horse and towards her. He started to say that they needed to go before the video started again. This time it was a young woman on the video telling Bry the same things, except that it would help him build muscle and get the "attention he deserved."

"What do you think about that?" she asked.

"Seems pretty convenient," he responded.

"There's gotta be something wrong with it."

On the way home, Ceres asked about the corn. "Does Cane sell his corn for fuel?" she asked.

"No, he sells it to a cannery across state lines," he replied. "Why d'you ask?"

"Just wondering where he sold his crops."

"It's a different type of corn that they can turn into fuel. There are entirely different guidelines set up from the government." Ceres looked to him to elaborate. "They don't like certain sprays bein' used. They don't use sweet corn. The soil has to have certain nitrates. It's real expensive to start making, so Cane decided against it a couple years back." Ceres nodded her head to show that she understood what he was talking about. "It would cost him thousands to convert his farm, so he didn't. Even though, long term, it would make him more money."

"I guess he didn't care cause he didn't have any kids he'd give the farm to. Maybe he thought he would die before he saw any of the benefit of the changeover," she said

Bry seemed distracted, "I guess."

His last words led her to suspect what he had been hiding all along. "You want to inherit the farm," she said.

Bry looked at her and said all he needed to say.

"In that case, you should stay," she added.

"If I can turn around some of the debt, it'll stop the Foundation from takin' it when Cane passes."

"I hope you do," she said after some thought.

"I'll let you know when he dies and maybe you can come back," he said with a smile.

She smiled back, but she knew that she would never go back to that place.

Deuteronomy 22:9

"Do not plant two kinds of seed in your vineyard; if you do, not only the crops you plant but also the fruit of the vineyard will be defiled."

When they returned to the farm, Bry suggested that they take a look at Aster's corn plant before the sun was gone. They left the groceries in the truck at the back of the house and went to the fields. The corn rows were full now. They were alive with uniform rows of corn husks.

"Pull your sleeves down," he said, "don't touch anything with your arms in case the spray hasn't set in."

She rolled down her sleeves and walked to where they had marked the blue seed.

Ceres looked up at Bry, "I think Aster died because of that spray."

Bry laughed, "The one that they just delivered *yesterday*? Aster died because she was old, not because of the spray. She lived longer because of the spray."

Ceres scrunched her face, "I don't get your logic."

"The spray isn't bad. Stop thinking about it so much. You would die without it."

Ceres thought *they were dying with it.*

After inspecting the ground in the rows, they came to the plant that had a ring of leftover pot circling its roots. They stood at the edge of the field with the plant in front of them.

"It looks no different from the rest," she said.

"Sure doesn't."

She reached for the ear and pulled down one of the sides by its silk without pulling it off of the plant. Underneath the coarse encasing, the most beautiful blue and green corn kernels made an appearance. The blue kernels were cerulean and the green were the color of algae. They were imperfect and ranged in size. One row had two blue to one large green and one small green. There was no definitive pattern to their ordinance. The next row was entirely different.

"That's peculiar," he said.

"I didn't know they made blue corn. Is this what they use for fuel?"

"Maybe," he said, "I don't know."

As they were inspecting the corn, the wind blew and Bry quickly covered her face and his own. She could feel the dirt hitting her face as she shut her eyes tightly. When the wind stopped, they opened their eyes again.

"Wash your face when you get home," he said sternly. She scrunched her brow.

Bry took the ear into his hand and pulled down the husk farther to reveal, what looked like, an entirely different ear of corn. The bottom of the corn, near the stalk, was golden yellow, uniform in its line and it appeared as if it was struggling to shape the top of the ear of corn.

"This is crazy!" he said. "We've got to go." He broke off the ear of corn and carried it back to his truck while

Ceres followed. She had too many questions for so few answers.

"Bry, what is happening? What is wrong with that plant? Is it sick? Why is it blue and not yellow?"

Bry didn't have any answers and he slammed the door of the truck after placing the corn inside. They heard another truck door slam at the front of the house. "Who is that?"

They crept over to the side of the house to see that Mort had returned. This time, he and his lady accomplice had forgotten their Western get up and wore grey suits and ties.

"What are they doin' here again?" Bry whispered.

Then, down the road into the farm, a large white van barreled down the road, kicking up dirt behind. It unloaded several men with white contamination suits creating a stark contrast with their black machine guns.

"What the hell is happening?" Bry said urgently.

"We've gotta leave," she said. "They're going to kill us. We have to leave, now."

Bry didn't know what to do. He didn't know if they should leave or if that made them *look* guilty. They peeked their heads to the window to see Cane open the front door of the farmhouse at the request of Mort's loud knock.

"Mr. Mort!" he said swinging a beer in his hand, "I don't need any more spray. I've got some left over from today. Covered the whole field."

Mort's lady friend pushed her way into the house. "We're not here about the spray Cane," her voice was no longer sweet, but deep and severe. Her hair was no longer tied back into a loose side ponytail, but a slicked back hairstyle that revealed her older age.

The army of suited men appeared on the porch behind Mort.

"What the hell are you here for then?" Cane said in alarm.

"Where did you get the seed?" Mort asked.

Ceres and Bry looked at each other with widened eyes.

"We gotta leave now, Bry!" Ceres whispered with persistence. "My bag is in your car already, let's go!"

"I bought all my seed from you," Cane said turning to look at the lady who was going through all of the books on the fireplace mantle. "What are you lookin' for?" he asked in a feeble voice.

"Your farm sent us a signal of a rare seed that you did not buy from us, Mr. Cane," Mort said in a nonchalant manner. "You can't be growing things that aren't approved. It's dangerous."

Cane was in shock.

"When our seed was created, Cane, it was made to express the genes we wanted. It suppressed the genes we didn't. Lastly, the real amazing feat, it lets us know when it has been cross-pollinated by an un-engineered organism."

"I don't do *un-engineered*, you know that," he said like it was a dirty word.

The men ran out onto the field at Mort's command and he continued into the house with his shiny white smile and crows-footed eyes.

Bry and Ceres quietly slid into the truck.

"Don't turn the lights on, they'll see us from the front of the house," she said.

"They're gonna hear the engine turn over," he replied.

Ceres turned to look out the back of the truck. She saw long streams of light, bending over the corn fields, finding their way around the house from the strobe lights of the men in suits.

"It doesn't matter, if we don't leave now we're dead."

Bry pushed in the clutch and the engine roared.

"Someone else here?" the lady said as she raised her eyebrow.

"Ceres!" Cane said as if he had the answer to the hardest question. "That damn girl must've planted the seeds you're talkin' about." Mort lifted his head up to tell a guard to go check out the back of the house. "My niece. She's been nothin' but trouble."

"Why is she here?" Ladybelle snapped.

"Needs parents for a few months," Cane said back.

"This isn't good," Mort said sitting down. "This is *not* good." He snapped his fingers to the lady next to him as she handed him some paper from her inside chest pocket. "You know what this is?" he said crossing his legs and leaning back in the chair.

Cane shook his head *no.*

"This is your contract. And you know what your contract says?"

He shook his head again.

"It says that you are not allowed to plant any type of dangerous foreign seed in tandem with your contracted seed, lest our seeds be pollinated with your *dangerous* foreign seed." Mort straightened his tie and cocked his head. "You planted a dangerous foreign seed so let's look at what happens to those who break their contracts." He started to flip to the back of the packet.

Cane started to shake his head violently. "No! I didn't break the contract, it was the girl. The girl broke the contract. I've never seen any seed but the ones that you sold me. I've done everything right."

The guard came back into the room. "Gone" he said and put his hand on Cane's shoulder, guiding him into the seat. The woman pulled out her pistol and put it to his temple.

"Where is she?" the lady said.

"Ladybelle," Mort said softly, "We're not going to kill him, today." He stood up. "Listen here, Cane. We're gonna need the girl and whatever seeds she has left. She comes back here, you turn her in, since she's your responsibility. If you deliver on that, we'll forget about some of these consequences. Sound alright?" He smiled so wide that his lips opened and showed the sides of his teeth.

Cane swallowed and wet his lips. "Deal."

Bry and Ceres travelled off of the farm and onto the paved road, this time away from town.

"Why is your bag in here? Did you know this was going to happen?" he asked.

Ceres was shocked, "No! How was I supposed to know that they were going to come with guns? It was your idea to plant that seed. Did you know this was going to happen?"

"Don't be ridiculous," he said. "I didn't want this, you did."

"Then drop me off and go back," she returned.

"Okay, I'll go back to the farm with a bunch of sciencey looking freaks with machine guns and just see what happens. Sounds like a good plan," he said.

"None of this is my fault," she said.

"You had the seeds, Ceres. And now they're gonna kill Cane and take the farm."

Ceres shook her head and looked out the window. "Don't we have bigger problems than whose fault it is that Cane is probably dead at the farm? Like where the hell are we going to go?"

Bry had no idea.

Ceres woke up when the car stopped. She saw the fluorescent lights of the fueling station above her and looked over at Bry.

"Need money?" she yawned.

"I've still got Cane's card," he said.

"I'm gonna go get a drink," she said back.

The cashier was a teenager with long black hair and a half-grown beard. He wore a beanie pulled over his eyebrows. He didn't get up from his chair that he was sitting in and leaned back against the wall.

"Sup," he said, stoned out of his mind.

She smiled, "Sup," she echoed and laughed.

She went down the aisle to the refrigerated beverages and picked up a soda and water.

When she took it to the counter, the teenager stood up from his chair.

"Whoa!" he said. "You're like, a fugitive?"

Ceres didn't know what to say, "What?" He pointed at the screen above her head and there she was in a picture from her senior Halloween party where she had dressed as a militant as a joke.

"What?" she said under her breath. She reached over the counter to the remote and unmuted the television:

Ceres Dixon and Bry Harrold are on the run now, with toxic chemicals that are hazardous to the environment. They are flippantly and recklessly using the biomatter to terrorize farms in the area. Dixon is a minor and has possibly been kidnapped by Harrold. If you have any informa...

"Thanks," she said as she gave him some money and briskly walked to the car.

"Gotta go, Bry," she said hopping into the cab. "Now."

Bry sped out of the station and headed north. He was mad. He was angry. He didn't like Ceres at that moment and he didn't like being pushed around.

"Why was your bag already in my car?" he demanded.

"I was going to leave from town last night. I thought you would want to go with me," she said meekly.

Bry scoffed, "Why didn't you leave then?"

"I thought I could change your mind after a few days, I guess."

Bry started laughing hysterically, "How is it possible for a person to be so smart and so dumb at the same time?"

Ceres's face turned sour. "That's not nice."

Bry felt bad, "I'm sorry." She didn't accept it. "Serious, I'm sorry. You aren't dumb. I just thought you knew that was my place and I wasn't gonna leave it for anything, even a girl."

"I'm so sick of being called a girl. It's like I grew up and then went back to fifth grade on the farm. No more calling me *girl*, it's seriously annoying."

Bry remained silent for the next few minutes before getting Cane's card out of his pocket. "What should we do with this?"

Ceres took it from him and threw it out the window. "This," she said.

Bry was shocked.

"They'll track it. They know where we are now. They know we went to that gas station, even if that stoner doesn't call the police on us."

Silence.

"I should wait to tell you this cause you're already mad at me, but maybe you should get all the mad out now."

Bry waited for the news.

"We were on TV. In the station. They said that we were fugitives. They showed our pictures." Ceres suddenly regretted her Halloween costume that year. She didn't mention the possibility of being kidnapped.

Bry hit the steering wheel with the palms of his hands over and over again, shouting swear words at the top of his lungs. Then he grasped the wheel until his knuckles turned white. His mouth was shut tightly and then he made a sharp and rigid turn off the road and stopped.

Ceres sat the same way, with her legs crossed and playing with the cap of her soda in her fingers.

"What are the seeds? Where are they? What did Aster tell you?" The way that he asked the questions made Ceres fear him, a real fear that trumped the materialized one which consumed her by the river.

"She said 'this will be your food'," Ceres said.

"That's it? This will be your food? Not, *this will screw you over*? Not, *this will ruin your life and Cane's life and the farm and cause people with machine guns to come after us*?"

She shook her head. "They were in the back of her Bible. And, when Cane went through her room after she died, he looked there. I know because he ripped the pages and it was all messed up on the floor. He went through her room like he was looking for them. I know that Cane knows what they are."

Bry calmed down as she spoke. He could hear the tremble in her voice and felt bad that he had caused it, especially because he had been trying so arduously to protect her. "Well we can't ask him now, and she's dead. Do you know anyone else that could have any idea what the hell we're supposed to do with them?"

Ceres thought through everyone she used to know. She thought through all of her courses, all of her teams and acquaintances. "Yes," she said. "Go east."

"I'm sorry," she said out of nowhere.

"Why? You don't have nothing to be sorry for. I'm the one that yelled at you," he replied.

"I'm sorry I expected you to leave. You made it pretty obvious that you really didn't want this, and even though we aren't in the best situation, it's closer to what I wanted than what you did. So, I'm sorry."

"Let's just figure it out. And then maybe they'll let us go home."

Bry realized that she didn't have a home and that maybe he should apologize for not understanding why she wanted to leave and for him to go with her. He should have been flattered. In any other circumstance, he would have been elated to have someone like Ceres want to run away with him. But it was the unknown destination that bothered him. He wanted the farm, and he knew that once Cane was gone, Bry was the closest to a son he had, so he was likely to inherit it, if he stayed in Cane's good graces. Bry didn't want to explain all of that either. It seemed callous; waiting for someone to die so that you could take their possessions. It seemed even worse that he was brown-nosing someone he didn't like, someone not even in his family, to weasel into a will.

"Don't say you're sorry again. We can't live life being sorry," he concluded.

They talked about disguises and whether or not they wanted to dye their hair or if Ceres should cut all of hers off. At the suggestion of chopping her hair, she looked uneasy.

"I'd rather just dye it, black maybe? I'll cut some bangs? Bangs always make people look totally different. I'll get some glasses?" She stopped, "Please don't make me cut it all off."

"Here's the deal, Ceres. You do what you want and I'll do what I want, but whoever gets both of us caught because their disguise isn't good enough has to volunteer to be shot first. Deal?"

Ceres laughed her real laugh again. "Deal. What are you going to do?"

"I'm going to shave my head. And this?" he said rubbing the five o'clock shadow on his face, "I'm gonna let it grow."

Ceres thought he had it easy.

She pulled out one of the noodle packets from the grocery bag at her feet. "You hungry?" she asked.

"Ya, let me just get out my kettle," he joked.

Ceres ripped open the bag at the top and emptied the contents of the seasoning packet over the noodles. She folded the opening shut again before vigorously shaking the bag.

"It's called prison ramen," she laughed as she handed him a broken off piece.

"I suppose we should get used to it," Bry smiled back.

Bry wore a low baseball cap as he checked into the motel. It had fluorescent lights and an hourly rate, so they knew that it wouldn't be likely that they were too concerned with fugitives.

They would only stay a few hours, which would cost them twice as much as a full night, so he said they would be there until morning.

The lady at the desk was old and had long, blond, over-curled hair with thick black roots. Lines grew from her mouth in all directions from her constant pucker around a cigarette.

"Just me and the wife," Bry said. Then he thought for a minute, "Two beds please. I mean, we're not married *yet* and..."

She nodded. "Don't ask, don't tell honey," she said handing him the keys. "Just don't set the place on fire."

Ceres put on gloves that felt like they were covered in flour. She mixed the tar colored goop into the white lotion and replaced the cap. She shook the mixture violently until it was fully amalgamated. She thought *here goes nothing* and squirted the potion down the white part in her hair. She pressed down the cold pigment on her scalp and felt a shiver go down her body. Her auburn hair disappeared under the substance. She would lift areas of her hair to reveal a spot or two that she had missed and started to panic that she would have a large gap at the back of her head, a large brunette clump that would reveal her secret. It wouldn't give away that she was pretending to be someone else, but it would be a tell that she wasn't very good at doing her own hair.

After all of the mixture was in, she massaged her head to make sure that it had made it into every nook and cranny. She looked at the black against her complexion and thought that this was, perhaps, a bad choice. She took her hair into a ponytail and spun it around into a self-contained bun on top of her head. She pulled the gloves off inside out so she wouldn't get any on her skin. She thought about doing her makeup darker to match her hair. She picked up the black brow/eyeliner she had purchased at the store and darkened her eyebrows. She drew a beauty mark on her right cheek and pretended like she was Marilyn Monroe before wiping it off with a tissue.

Bry knocked at the door, which startled her. "Can I use that room?" he said.

She looked at her spread of hair color, makeup, clothes and toiletries in the room and then at the state of her face and hair in the mirror.

"Um," she clamored, trying to tidy things, "Give me just a minute."

She buttoned up the shirt she was wearing and pulled on some pajama pants before opening the door.

"Whoa," he said walking in and shutting the door.

She was embarrassed and she heard him say, "stinks in here," through the door. She heard the toilet flush and when he came out he said, "Your face is dripping." She brushed the drip away with the back of her hand and then swore, running into the bathroom to wash it off with soap. It was too late though, and the brown streak had stained her skin. It matched the tops of her ears and around the peaks of her forehead.

Ceres reluctantly stepped into the dingy shower after the twenty minutes her hair took to take the dye. The water was warm, but every once in a while it would heat to the point of scalding, causing her to step out from under the water quickly, risking the chance of slipping on the tub.

The color ran down her shoulders and she clamped her eyes shut to avoid any dye getting into her eyes. She allowed the water to push her hair into her face. She spit out the water that ran down her cheeks and into her mouth. When she figured it had been enough time, she slicked her hair back and opened her eyes. She looked at the drain and tried to decipher if the water had run clear, but couldn't tell against the grimy stain of the tub. She collected all of her hair and squeezed it with one hand while collecting the water with the other.

Clear.

Afterwards, Ceres took the towel off of her head to feel the straw-like black strands it revealed. She took the pick-comb and ran through her hair from the bottom to the roots. After she had broken her hair at all of the split ends, she brushed it as she always had one last time before parting it in the middle and pulling out the chunk of hair in the front that would become her new bangs. She didn't want bangs. She had them when she was a child. Her mom had cut them for her and they made her feel little again. As she snipped the scissors across her hair, she longed for her mother. She cut straight across and tried not to cry. She wouldn't cry because Bry would think it was about her hair, even if she explained it was not.

When Ceres came out, Bry was laying on his bed with his head against the backboard and his legs straight and crossed at the ankles.

He looked up and stared at her.

"You look so different."

"Good," she said.

"No, really. You look so different."

"Perfect, then you'll be the one that gets us caught."

Bry kept staring at her as she moved around the room, touching her hair. She hated the feel of it, but knew that it would get better with a few more washes. Only, she didn't know when she would be able to wash her hair again. "Your turn to do the deed," she laughed throwing him the razor.

"I don't think I'll bic it," he said. "I think I'll look weird bald."

"Well I thought *I'd* look weird…"

"You do look weird."

"Thanks, you're such a gentleman."

He laughed and got up from the bed, "Wanna help?"

She did, because she had never shaved a person's head before, but she hesitated thinking about cutting his head open and envisioned blood rolling down his face. "You'll be okay."

Ceres couldn't help but pull her bangs down her face; she thought that maybe she could grow them out by pulling on them like a doll she had as a girl, like her head was just filled with spools of new hair, waiting for a bad haircut. It didn't work. She pulled down the comforter of the bed and sat on the sheets; a trick her mother taught her when they'd stayed in hotels. Though, her parents would have never stayed in a dive like this. Her mother would say that cleaning ladies would never wash comforters, only sheets, so it was better to not use anything but the sheet. Ceres looked at the sheet and was skeptical that these had been washed either. They were a sky blue that matched the Southwest décor of the room.

She turned on the television to see cartoons, then a Marlon Brando movie, then the news, where her and Bry's faces were plastered in the top right corner.

She said, "Catch me now," under her breath.

Bry swung open the door and leaned on the frame. His head was white and shiny, backlit in the light with obvious areas in the back that he couldn't reach easily and therefore sliced. He had managed to stick toilet paper on the cut to stop the bleeding, but he looked hysterical.

She smiled, "Lookin' good."

He strut across the room. "It'll look even better with my full beard in a few days."

"Don't you think that'll look weird? A shaved head with a beard?"

"We aren't trying to look attractive. We're trying to not draw attention to ourselves. We're trying to look like someone else."

Bry did look like someone else. He looked like a teacher Ceres had been in love with at boarding school. He was a writer, a poet. He spoke with a strong Southern accent. She admired him, wanted his approval miserably. He made her want to be a writer, encouraged her to keep it writing. He had passed away a week after she graduated in some sort of car accident and she heard about it in the airport on her way to the farm. She cried on the plane and the lady next to her comforted her about the flight and said it wasn't "gonna go down," which only made her cry more.

"Bry," she started. He looked up from watching the television. "How do you know about Vera's Bar? Is it because you go there?" As soon as she heard the words come out of her mouth she regretted them. "You know, to…you know."

Bry smiled a little, "no."

He studied the map at the desk in the motel room as Ceres slept on top of the sheets. He circled all the places he knew he could go, which were few, and crossed out all the places that they should avoid. Ceres had told him that they were going to Gianesburg in the foothills, that she knew someone there that would know what the seeds were and how to help them. There was only one road close to them into the town and it was the same road that went through the Foundation Estates. They figured that it was better to risk going through the homes of the Foundationers than to spend days, and fuel, trying to go the round-a-bout way.

Bry slept for a few hours after Ceres got up. They laughed when she got out of bed and left a black ring on her pillowcase where her head had been.

At four, before the sun had risen, Ceres and Bry dropped the key at the front desk's receptacle and made their way northeast to her friend, Sege. He had taken AP Biochem in school, and college courses too. He was the smartest person Ceres knew. He came up with things Ceres never understood, but he was the best ping pong partner that she ever had.

They stopped at an offbeat traditional gas station where Bry traded his truck for an older four-wheel drive Bronco. The man at the station thought it was a steal, in his favor. It probably was, as this car had sticky gears and trouble running on the corn fuel. It had been a traditional SUV that had been converted to be efficient. In the transition, it had changed the integrity of the engine. He said, "Most cars just need you to ride it out."

Bry was sad to see his truck disappear in the rearview.

"It's for the best," she said patting his shoulder awkwardly.

"I've had that truck for years," he replied. "Dad's had that truck for years."

She patted his shoulder once more before gracefully crossing her legs and looking out the window. She reached to roll the window up manually and found that it stopped four inches from the top. She looked at Bry with a grin, "I miss the truck too."

The man who sold his Bronco for a deal got more than he bargained for when he turned in a tip that the car that the police were looking for had shown up on his property. They came and threw him a couple hundred dollars for the information and hauled off the truck. Even though he turned in the tip, he didn't tell them what kind of car they took in exchange. Actually, he did, but the wrong type. He didn't know why. He started to say that it was a crimson Bronco, but instead he thought about their youth, how kind Bry had been, and said it was a blue Blazer. Once he said it, he didn't want to correct himself for fear the authorities think he was a liar and lock him up. He could, however, tell them which direction they headed.

Ceres saw a family of four, a mother and three children, sitting at the bus stop on the side of the road. They looked like they were wearing clothes from the past. They were turquoise and purple, sweatpants and mismatched socks and shoes. The lady smiled as Bry slowed down to the town's speed limit and Ceres half-smiled back.

"Hey," he said to Ceres, "I meant to give you this." He reached into his pocket and pulled out a gold chain with a quarter size pendant in the shape of a square cube.

"What is this?" she said surprised.

"It was Aster's. I found it in her room when I was staying there. I thought you might want to have it before Cane could pawn it." She untangled the chain and put it around her neck.

"Thanks," she said quietly. "That's amazing." The road went from dilapidated and rough to smooth and clear when they reached the county line. It was as if they measured exactly where to cut off funding for the streets. Ceres hadn't experienced such a great dichotomy before. She knew that poverty lived directly adjacent to wealth, but she hadn't seen it and so it wasn't real to her. The grass went from dead to green and children played on white cement sidewalks where there were only pebbles before.

"It's like we're driving into another world," she said.

"I didn't know it was really this bad," he said back. "Now you're all decked out," he said. Ceres shook her head like she didn't know what he meant. "I mean with your fancy gold ring and now your necklace. I could just drop ya off here and you'd fit right in."

Ceres looked down at her clothes and laughed. "Do all of these people work at the Foundation?" she asked.

Bry nodded. All of the families had some connection to the Foundation. Some were grandfathered in and lived off of their inheritance; others had arduously worked their way up in the company to retire in the town. People waved at them, even though they were in an old car surrounded by shiny new Cadillacs and BMWs. They seemed nice enough; they shared the same glassy smiles as Mort, who she was sure was on their tails. It was only a matter of time before they were caught with seeds in their hands.

The houses were large and had sloped roofs like an alpine village. It was popular now, but in a few years it would be replaced by the next new trend. There were houses being built in the middle of already established neighborhoods, likely where outdated houses had been scraped and new models were being installed.

Past the town, the green grass stopped and the road became bumpy again. It was as if they had slipped into an alternate universe and slipped back out again; no one noticed, no one cared.

They headed up into the foothills as the sun began to set on their second day as runaways. Somehow, 48 hours seemed both shorter and longer. It was easier and harder than being on the farm. There were things that they missed and new things that they loathed.

Ceres squinted her eyes. "There, turn right," she said as they approached a hidden dirt road.

"You've been here before?" he asked.

"No. Sege just told me about it. He said that everyone always misses the turn." She looked around to the sign that could only be seen if you were coming down the mountain. "Yep, Willowed Road. This is it."

Although she knew that this was their intended destination, she didn't know what they would find when they arrived, and the thought made her uneasy. Naturally her mind went to the worst that Mort and his friends had known that they would go to Sege's and that they were waiting for them there. Or, that Mort had killed Sege for information on his old friend. She envisioned the scene, like she always did, and then shook her head and said something inane to Bry to change the thoughts in her mind.

Ceres worried that they had made a wrong turn when they hit a patch of aspen trees and the road disappeared.

"Are you sure this is the right road?" Bry asked coming to a stop.

Ceres shook her head, "I don't know, yes? I was sure he said *Willowed Road*." She got out and walked a few yards from the car. She looked at the ground and though she didn't see any tire marks, she did see the imprints of horse's hooves making their way to the right and through the woods.

"It's here," she said. "We have to walk."

Bry pulled the car around the other side of a nearby hill to hide it from the view of the road before getting Ceres's bag out of the back. He lifted the strap over his head so it rested across his chest. She said a quick 'thanks' before following the tracks.

"What if you're tracking a wild horse?" he laughed.

"I'm so happy you can laugh in this situation," she said stepping ankle deep into a pile of mud. Bry laughed out loud, a hearty laugh that seemed to echo down the valley. She turned around and scolded him with her eyes then tried to hide her own amusement at the predicament by turning towards the path again.

They followed the tracks in the mud through the aspens that glistened with the last remaining rays of sunlight from the day. Ceres tried to appreciate the scenery, but she couldn't breathe in fully. There was always a bit of room at the bottom of her lungs that she wouldn't let fill up with air. She had to purposefully breathe all the way in and all the way out every once in a while, but then she would forget again and breathe in short, staccato breaths. She couldn't help but feel as if someone was watching them. She turned quickly to look behind her when a snap of branches sounded as if it was coming from an outside source, but there was nothing to be seen. They were alone.

When the aspens broke, they arrived at a wooden cabin on a large, open piece of land. There was nothing around for miles. There was smoke billowing out of the stacked chimney and two black horses tied to a wooden hitching post on the edge of the driveway that had showed up magically out of nowhere.

Ceres looked at Bry and he looked back as if to tell her that she was right about the horses, and the house, when she stopped.

"Let's go," he said walking past her.

She thought: *What if he's not here? What if that's someone else with the fire? What if that fire is burning all the evidence of his life there and heating the pitchforks that will be used to chase us back down the aspen grove?*

Ceres kept walking. She knew that anything that she said to Bry would just be made fun of, and since they were already there, they might as well just check.

She remembered Sege as nice. He had had a thing for her their freshman year, a thing Ceres only returned in junior year when it was too late. It had never been the right time for either of them, and now was no exception. Besides being wanted by the police, Sege had a new girlfriend, so they hadn't spoken much in the last quarter of school. She was probably there with him and she didn't like Ceres very much. There were a lot of things that were filling her stomach with butterflies at the moment and she decided not to think about them. She forged through. The mud squished in her shoe. She walked briskly past Bry and up to the door as it opened immediately and a man with a zipped-up black hoodie pulled her inside. She grabbed Bry's arm to follow and the door slammed behind them.

"What are you doing here?" he said pushing off the hood of his sweatshirt to reveal a mess of shaggy brown hair.

Ceres was shocked. "I need help," she said.

He pulled a rifle out from behind the coat rack as Bry put his hands up to his sides. "Listen, I don't know how you got here, but you need to put your bag down and leave." He seemed to be shaking, but Ceres couldn't tell if it was from anger or fear.

"Sege," she said, "you're going to shoot me? It's Ceres."

"She's dead. You're an imposter."

"What?!" she said with her eyes wide.

"I just saw it on the news. They caught her and her friend and they are dead. The armed Occa shot them right on TV." He lifted the gun up and looked down the barrel to her face.

"I'm *really* not an imposter. How can I prove it? You're Sege Holland. You and I were in French class together until you were kicked out because you kept saying bad words."

"That's not enough," he said uneasy on his feet. "What other lies could you hear from any one of our classmates?"

Ceres racked her brain.

"Do you really think we're imposters?" Bry said. "That's straight out of a movie."

"Listen, guy. I saw a close up of Ceres and a dude that looked exactly like you get shot on the street when you tried to blow up the Foundation with some kind of homemade pipe bomb. So either you're imposters trying to get into my mind and my house, or they would have some reason for wanting everyone to think that you two are dead."

"Christmas break, junior year, I made you put on lipstick and kiss the back of my closet door," she blurted.

"I'm happy it's you, Ceres. But I'm pissed that you just said that out loud." He put the gun down and gave her a hug. "You're shaking," he said holding onto her.

"You just had a gun in my face," she said back, into his neck.

"This guy seems real nice," Bry said picking up her bag again.

"He doesn't have to be nice, Bry, just smart. We need your help, really need it," she said then looked around. "Alta here?"

Sege nodded. "And she's gonna hate that you are too, so let's just not wake her up."

"Why is she sleeping so early?"

"Late nap. We take shifts looking out for trespassers." He walked into the kitchen and poured himself a glass of whiskey from a fancy crystal decanter on the island.

Bry leaned over to Ceres, "This guy's a real nut." She elbowed him in the stomach.

"So you're going to talk to me about the seeds you stole, right? The bioterrorism?" he said sitting at the island.

"We didn't steal anything. We didn't know what the seeds were or where they came from. We were hoping that you could help us figure it out."

"Well," he said lifting his arms up in a stretch over his head, "Do you want to know what they are saying about you?"

"Do we?" Bry said curiously.

"Well first of all, Ceres is a whore. She tried to seduce her own uncle to take over the farm and plant the seeds that she stole from the bio lab at Atkins. Atkins, by the way, isn't necessarily on board with this, but they are considering revoking your degree, due to pressure from the media. They also released all of your school records to SNX News. You probably didn't want to get arrested for that joint junior year, because they really are using that to show how much of an extremist you are; your Halloween costume didn't help. They have ideas about you having a mental breakdown because of your parents' deaths. They seem to think that you have nothing to live for, so you're willing to die terrorizing the crops of the Midwest."

Ceres stood with her mouth wide open until she realized how she probably looked.

"And you, Bry is it? You are a dumb oaf that follows the lead of the whore that's using you as a scapegoat slash getaway driver. Of course, the news used some other choice words to describe the situation, but not to worry; you're yesterday's news as this morning you were caught sneaking into the Foundation with some hand grenades, so they killed you. They have video and everything. It was really convincing, but it always is. The Occa were there in swarms, ready to haul your bodies in."

"Sege is a little bit of a conspiracy theorist," she said to Bry.

"Um, excuse me. I'm not a theorist. I'm stating the facts. And what this situation right here says to me is that I've been right all along."

"Who are Occa?" Bry asked.

"Enforcers. They're the armed men and women of the Foundation. They're like bodyguards. Comes from the Greek myth of Occator, harrowers. The ones that break up the land, smooth out the soil. The guy that runs that place is real into shit like that."

Ceres and Bry knew that the Occa were at Cane's farm, trying to smooth over the mess of Aster'sseeds. They stood in the kitchen together in silence for a moment. Ceres shifted her weight. "No one is coming to my defense?" she asked angrily. "No one is saying that I would never do that?"

"Ceres..." Sege started. Ceres knew that no one wanted to implicate themselves. He changed the focus, "Would you like something? Live it up, the night is young." Ceres poured herself a glass of water from the pitcher and Bry did the same. They toasted to something or other and sat again at the island.

"So, do you have the seeds?" Sege asked with his hand out.

Ceres didn't know whether or not to show them to him. She didn't know if he could be trusted. It was clear that Bry wasn't sure of the situation either, but he reached into the side pocket of Ceres's bag and lifted out the husk of corn that they had grown from the seed.

Sege took it from his hand and peeled back the silk. He grabbed his horn-rimmed glasses from the table and put the corn right up to his face. He couldn't quite make out where the change happened, but he saw that the top of the cob was one color, one species of corn, and the other end was quite another.

"How did you do this?" he said placing the corn on the table and getting a bottle of ethanol from the cabinet.

"I told you, Sege. I don't know. It was from a seed that my aunt gave me before she died."

"This corn doesn't exist anymore, Ceres. That's why they're after you."

"Who is after us? Is it dangerous?" Bry urged.

"Can I?" he asked taking a knife out of a drawer. Ceres nodded knowing the rest of the seeds were safely in her bag and Sege cut the corn off of the cob in three sections. The first was entirely blue and green, the second yellow and golden, and the third the hybrid.

"It's not exactly orthodox, but I'm going to extract the DNA and analyze it."

"With alcohol?" Ceres asked.

"Yes, and a detergent. It's a party trick. I'm surprised you didn't see it in Colb's room. I used to do it there to end out the night," he said.

"Sure sounds like you guys had fun parties. DNA extractions and ping pong. You must have been the cool kids," Bry chuckled.

"Your friend thinks he's funny," Sege said while he brought out a makeshift kit with pipets and dyes. Ceres watched with wide eyes as Bry rummaged through the kitchen for something to eat. Sege cut the corn kernels off of each of the sections and into three separate mortar and pestles. Ceres thought it was strange that a person would have so many mortar and pestles, especially because she had only seen one once in her life and that was on a table at a restaurant to see the waiter make "homemade" guacamole.

Sege ground each of the samples into a gooey paste and put them into their own crystal shot glasses. He then got out the dish soap from under the sink and dropped a few squirts into each of the cups. He went back to the sink and filled a measuring cup with some warm tap water and poured a little into each of the cups. He mixed each of the mixtures slowly to avoid making bubbles and then poured himself another drink.

"Is that it?" she asked while beside her Bry chomped on a sandwich he'd helped himself to from the refrigerator.

"Five minutes and then we'll add the alcohol. Then I can extract the DNA. I'll need to take it into my dad's office to see if I can see any obvious differences in the genome."

Ceres walked around the room and looked at the books. Sege had followed in his father's footsteps with his interest in biochemistry but refused to accept the Foundation's offer to join their science team where they pay to have their studies' results fixed as they prefer. Because Sege declined their pushy offer, they made sure all of the competitors failed to review his applications. It nearly tore his family apart. Sege's mother moved into a large apartment on Foundation land with his father and sent money and a fresh grocery delivery every month to support him. His dad knew about it, but he didn't report it to his superiors. They would ask Sege every once in a while if he was willing to reconsider their offer. He always wrote back, respectfully declining the offer and posting it to a different friend in a different state each time to post back to the Foundation. They never knew that Sege was right under their noses, just right up the hill. He had confided in Ceres one night when he and Alta were fighting, a week before she left for the farm. That was why she didn't like Ceres; because Ceres knew secrets Alta didn't.

After five minutes, and another drink, Sege poured a measured amount of alcohol into each of the cups, releasing thousands of white strands that crawled up the sides of the glass and spiraled in the middle of the liquid.

"Beauty," he said.

"That's the DNA?" she asked.

"It's amazing," he responded.

He took a bent open paper clip and lifted the DNA from each of the cups and placed them individually from the cups onto their own microscope slide. He then covered them carefully with a coverslip.

"Your hands are pretty steady for being so drunk," Bry said staring.

"You don't know I'm drunk. You know nothing."

"Whoa," Ceres said after she breathed in, "don't start this."

Sege took the bottle and, without taking his eyes off of Bry, put it to his lips and took back another few gulps of the golden liquid.

Sege left the kitchen/room and headed to his father's office downstairs.

"I don't like this," Bry said in all seriousness to Ceres. "I think we should leave."

Ceres looked outside. "It's dark. I don't want to leave until morning."

"It's not that dark. I'll protect you. In all reality, it will be safer out there than in here."

"Well you can protect me in here. We can't leave. I need to know what we're doing next. Where'd we even go?"

"Anywhere, Ceres," he said moving towards her and putting his hand on her arm. "This is not safe. We are not safe with that guy."

She pulled her arm away from him, "You don't know him like I do. All he cares about is sticking it to "the man." The Foundation is the man. I didn't get it before, but he can help us. I wouldn't know what to do without him."

Bry slowly nodded his head and narrowed his eyes, "I'm leaving first thing tomorrow morning." He walked towards the couch, sat down and put his feet up on the coffee table.

"Don't do that," she said.

"I think this guy won't mind if I put my feet up on the table," he said kicking off the magazines onto the floor.

"Why are you acting like this? I thought we were in this together."

"Together would be making decisions," he paused, "together. All of this is your decision."

"Bry…"

"So tomorrow, I'll leave. That's my decision. And if you wanna come, you can. Or maybe we aren't in this *together* anymore."

Sege still hadn't come up from the office. It was getting late, and she wanted to know where she and Bry could sleep. She didn't want to talk to Bry so she wandered down the hall to the right of the foyer to see if there were any open doors. There weren't. The wooden floors squeaked beneath her feet, and sent shivers up her spine. She looked down the dark hallway, then back at the light from the foyer and the kitchen. She turned around again to the first door on the right. She put her hand on the doorknob. It was cold. She wrapped her fingers around the brass knob and heard the floor creak behind her. It was *only Bry,* she thought, as she turned to find a silver blade inches from her eyes. She screamed as the shadowed figure pushed her to the ground and pushed the knife towards her face.

"What the hell are you doing here?" the shadow screamed, "What do you want with us?" A shock of blond hair covered the assailant's face. Her body was small, but it was not weak. When she moved, her hair revealed the heart shape of her chin, the pink lip balm on her lips.

The knife hovered over her face and Ceres lost her strength, allowing the woman's hands to dip into her turned cheek. Alta looked her directly in the eye and didn't flinch.

Ceres couldn't scream or speak as Alta's knee pushed up her stomach and into her ribcage. Ceres could feel the blade enter her skin as she tried desperately to push Alta off of her. She shifted, only slightly. "Cer..." she mouthed. "Ceres." The blood from her cheek rolled up towards her eye and filled the socket with blood.

Alta's strength was too much for her but the blood in her eye sparked something in Ceres. She *wanted* to live. She didn't want to die in a hallway. She wanted answers. She couldn't die without knowing. She pushed with all she had, and Alta flew backwards towards the door. Ceres wiped her eye and closed it, crying tears of blood before grabbing an elk horn lamp from the end table and bashing it on Alta's hand, knocking the knife out of it.

Alta lunged towards her as Ceres screamed, "It's Ceres, you psycho!" and bashed her over the head. She fell to the floor with a thump as Bry came around the corner to see Ceres open her eye and wipe the blood across her face.

Ceres dropped the lamp and ran towards him, sidestepping the body in the hall and throwing her arms around him.

"She messed me up," she said pushing her cheek against his shirt. He pushed back her face to inspect the wound. "I need a bandage," she said with a quivering lip. He chuckled. She said, "She stabbed me," in the smallest way possible.

"This is not the time to tell you *I told you so,* but Ceres..." She kept holding onto him, putting pressure on her cheek and trying to blink out the blood from her eye.

Sege, Bry and Ceres stood at the end of the hallway staring at Alta's twisted body. Sege was too drunk and interested in his work to care that his girlfriend was, perhaps, dead in the corridor.

"Have you seen her move?" he asked.

She kicked out her leg at the sound of his voice.

"Yes," Ceres said.

Sege bobbed his head, "We should probably tie her up. She might get a little animated when she wakes up."

Ceres's face twisted in shock at the assertion, "Okay. Where's the rope?"

Sege got the rope from the garage and instructed them how to tie it so that she wouldn't really be hurt. They moved her to the bed in the first room and tied her hands together and to the back of the headboard.

They inspected her wound and Bry checked her pulse and her eyes. "She's out," he said.

"I'm happy I didn't kill her," Ceres said to them as they looked at her body on the bed.

"Me too, that would've been a real bummer," Sege said. "Keep the door open. Sorry about your face."

Ceres half-smiled. "I'm also happy she doesn't have access to a gun."

"Oh, she does. You're lucky she didn't see the back of your head and shoot."

Ceres thought that Alta must have known her face. Her hair was different, but maybe she had seen it was her and wanted to kill her. Alta would use the excuse that she didn't recognize Ceres, but the memory of seeing her and her fiancé share secrets under the stairs couldn't rub her face from Alta's mind.

"We'll leave in the morning," she said to Bry.

He just nodded and put his arm around her.

After Bry had closed his eyes for good that night, Ceres went over to her bag and pulled out the burlap pouch of seeds from the bottom. She slipped them into her jeans' pocket so that they were close to her. In the morning, they were awoken by the sunlight peering in through the window of the living room and Sege standing over them.

"It's heirloom," he said as they opened their eyes to him.

Ceres moved from the nook of Bry's open arm, "What does that mean?"

"It means they want it because it began the genome. It's what doesn't exist anymore. It is the original. It is what everything they have comes from."

Bry looked confused.

"They took those seeds, forever ago, maybe a hundred years," Sege said alluding to the blue seeds, "and they changed them. They changed so much, though, that they lost the originals. Bastardized them. They didn't think they would need the originals, perhaps. But in their changes the fields started to create toxins that attracted superbugs and super weeds. So they decided that they needed the originals. And when they showed up on your uncle's farm they knew that they had a chance to get back what they thought they had lost so many years ago."

"They are just seeds," Ceres said. "I can't understand why that's enough to kill anyone for."

"They aren't just seeds," Sege replied. "They could ruin the entire infrastructure of farming."

"Because they are free," Ceres started to understand why they were desperate to get their hands on them. She turned to Bry. "These seeds are coveted by the Foundation, but not by Adamemnon, or whatever that bug was called. Those crops that Cane had were from the Foundation, and the pesticides that he used were from the Foundation. He's stuck. But these," she said pulling out the pouch from her back pocket, "these are free. And they want them so we can't ruin their business."

Bry was starting to get why it was enough to kill for. If they grew the corn themselves and sold the seeds to the people that were trapped into buying whatever the Foundation wanted them to buy, they would slowly lose their customers, and money is everything.

"Sege, are the pesticides that they are using making people sick? Could that be why people are dying?" Ceres asked.

"It's that, and that these things aren't natural. Whatever you believe in, you know what was put here on earth was real, and it changed organically. It was masterful. It would resist certain diseases, it would change its own DNA to no longer be susceptible to certain conditions. What didn't survive, didn't survive. Then people started to get real mad. They wanted foods year-round that wouldn't grow normally in all seasons. They were angry that their favorite bananas were being destroyed by a rogue disease. So the Foundation started their own modifications. They crept into the DNA and clipped things, spliced the originals with characteristics from the new foods. And the people were happy. They didn't know that they had created a monster; that what they caused could never be undone. Sickness will never be tied to the foods that they altered, because there are too many other variables," Sege explained.

"So what do we do?" Bry said.

"You have to find a place that will allow you to grow these seeds. Then you need to give them to all of the people that can't do anything else but live under the omnipotent shadow of the Foundation," Sege said.

"That's just it, Sege. They are omnipotent. How did they know that we had even grown that seed on Cane's land? We didn't tell anyone and Cane had no idea when they showed up."

"Cross-pollination signals," he said after a minute. "Those seeds are designed to signal when they have pollinated a foreign organism. In most cases, the foreign organism is likely an organic, or "un-engineered" plant. They send signals back to the Foundation to let them know how they have affected the DNA of the host plant."

Ceres began to get suspicious of his answers. "Why do you know all of this, Sege?" she asked.

Sege hesitated to answer until she said it again, this time with a more serious tone.

"My dad invented it," he admitted. "I don't think he knew," he stopped, "what he was doing when he did. But now he can't get out."

"Anyone can get out of anything," she replied. "It doesn't matter, Sege. It doesn't matter what your dad did. It matters what you do."

"No," he said, "it matters what *you* do."

There was a knock and a moan. *Alta must be awake,* they thought, and she was. It was only a matter of seconds before she realized that she had been tied to the bed and started panicking.

The threesome went towards the room but Sege held back Ceres and Bry in the hallway to go in alone.

"What the hell is going on, Sege? Why did you tie me?" her voice whined.

Sege shh'ed her and said, "Listen, Alta. Ceres and Bry are here."

"What?" she whispered. "Who did I stab in the hallway?"

"Ceres," he said back.

"I don't like her," she whispered. "Did she die?"

Ceres made a face in the hallway.

"No, she's still here. She's good. She's with someone else who is good, too," Sege explained.

Alta looked out to the hallway. "Are they out there? In the hall? Come in here; I know you're here," she shouted.

Ceres and Bry walked into the room. She folded her arms, and he smiled awkwardly.

Alta looked away, “Sorry about your face. It looks really bad.”

“That sounds sincere,” Ceres responded. “Sorry about hitting you over the head when you tried to kill me and tying you to the bed,” she said in like sincerity.

Alta rolled her eyes, “Why am I still tied up? Can you do something about this please?” she insisted.

Sege moved to untie her when they heard a loud knock at the door.

“Who is that?” Bry asked.

Sege left the bedroom and put his finger over his mouth to quiet the others. He grabbed the rifle from the foyer and put his ear on the door. The knock happened again and it startled him.

“Who is it?” he said in his deepest voice.

“Grocery Delivery,” the voice replied.

“Leave it at the door,” he said.

“You have to sign,” the voice persisted.

He opened the door to see a man on the ground and a pistol in his face.

“Sign right here, Sege,” Ladybelle said.

“That doesn’t even make sense,” he said “You don’t have anything for me to sign.”

She looked to her right and signaled another person. Mort came around the corner.

“Hey little buddy!” he said. “You can always sign the papers at the Foundation, the same contract your daddy did maybe?”

Bry and Ceres heard the shot and Alta screamed.

They hurriedly opened the window and Bry helped Ceres jump out first.

Mort gave the signal for the same armed men to infiltrate the house as did the farm. The first few stepped over Sege's body, the last few helped drag it to one of the vans on the lawn outside of the cabin.

The Occa rounded the hallway corner to find Alta, half-tied to the bed and screaming.

"They went out the window," she screamed.

As soon as Ceres's feet hit the ground she sprinted towards the aspen grove. She heard footsteps behind her and was sure it was Bry until she was tackled to the ground. The body hit her back and pummeled her to the grass. She kicked both legs of her attacker and rolled away from the dark figure. She looked back at the house where she saw Bry being taken down before his feet hit the ground.

She scrambled to get up again, and did. The coercer got up and followed her again, but with a shorter gait. And she entered the grove.

The morning sunlight left the aspens glimmering. Each green leaf was amplified into a silver sliver of green snow that hung from the canopy. It was beautiful and she recognized it in her terror. She ran, dodging through the trees and slipping over fissures in the landscape. She looked back briefly to see that she had not lost her follower, as she could see her farther back, but she was gaining ground. She had lost Bry and knew her only hope would be to get to the car on the other side of the coppice.

She could see the end. She didn't look back again and broke through the trees to see Mort and the Occa from the farm. She stopped immediately. With evil in front and behind she opened her body to the side to try to see as many of them as possible.

Her chest heaved, gasping for air. All guns were drawn on her.

"I've long sought you, my dear," Mort said. "Put her in."

She stepped backwards towards the vehicle.

"Don't make this ugly," he said. "I don't want to have to hurt you. I'm here to help."

She stopped, only momentarily, and was taken by the hands behind her and led to the van.

She was parceled into the back cargo hold of the van. Two of the Occa sat on the opposite side, in front of her. The front row of seats was sectioned off with a partition that lowered to reveal Mort, his face sectioned into squares by the wire grid that separated them.

"Let's make a deal," he said.

Ceres said, "No, thanks" and stared at the wall in between the guards.

"You aren't really in any position to *not* make any kind of deal, dear," he said.

She looked into his eyes, "You're going to kill me, so what kind of deal would I be making? One that decides how I'm going to die? Or one that barters my friends' lives for the lives of others? I don't want anything to do with dangerous men."

Mort shut the partition angrily. He opened it seconds later to Ceres still staring at him. "You are the danger here. You are the one that deserves to die. Don't let others suffer for your ignorance."

"I don't know what you're talking about. I'm no danger."

"You don't know what you have in your hands, or your bag or wherever you stashed those seeds. You are a terrorist. A terror. You are more of a danger than I'll ever be." And the partition closed again. This time it stayed shut. One of the Occa slapped some handcuffs on her and they sat in silence.

They travelled for hours, it seemed. The hot sun boiled the top of the vehicle and there was no air conditioning in the hollow hold of the van.

Ceres, noticing the female Occa's sweat rolling down from under her helmet, said, "You can take your helmet off."

The Occa looked blankly back at her.

"Marta, your name is?"

The guard didn't blink.

"I heard them say it earlier. You can take it off. I can't attack you or anything," she said holding up her handcuffed hands. "Plus Bruno over here'd take me down at the first move."

"His name's not Bruno," she said and he shoved her.

"Uh oh, sorry," Ceres said, "I was just trying to help."

Luke 9:23-24

"Then he said to them all: 'Whoever wants to be my disciple must deny themselves and take up their cross daily and follow me. For whoever wants to save their life will lose it, but whoever loses their life for me will save it.'"

Ceres's head rolled and hit the front divider when the car abruptly stopped. She took her bound hands and wiped the hair off her brow. Then she wished she had a mirror, to check the wound on her face.

"Get up," Marta said.

Ceres did as she said. She was happy to have slept, however uncomfortably. She stood up with a bent spine in the cargo hold. Marta and the other Occa stood hunched, ready to deploy.

The doors opened to reveal a grey parking garage and Mort standing with his small lady friend, Ladybelle. She saw the other van but it was empty.

"Where is Bry?" she asked.

"He's none of your concern," Ladybelle said.

"Yes, he is. Where is he?" she pushed.

"Let's not start out like this, dear. Let's start again as friends," Mort said, signaling the Occa to take off her handcuffs. "See," he said, "friends. That is, until you try to run away, or escape. That would make us look bad, because we told the world you were dead, and we can't let you ruin our reputation."

Ceres snarled.

"We'll get you some medical help for your cheek. That must've been painful."

"I didn't feel a thing," she lied.

"I'm happy you are so tough," Marta said under her breath to her. "You will need to be."

Ceres was taken to the oversized elevator. Mort held his hands in front of him, holding one of his wrists with his other hand. He looked straight ahead at their frosted reflections in the silver doors as they closed. Ceres pulled at her bangs.

"They look nice, Ceres," he said leaning over. "I must say, they threw us off at first, not being able to tell if it was you in your new car with our cameras. Your friend's disguise was far less convincing, which is actually what discovered you."

She smiled a little then stopped. She didn't know if Bry was alive and it seemed wrong to gloat, even if it was only in her mind. The elevator stopped and the doors opened to the clinic.

Mort looked over at her, "This is where you get out. I'll be seeing you around."

Ladybelle and Marta ushered Ceres to the infirmary. They walked into the cavernous and blazingly white room to a counter with a lady wearing a nursing cap.

"Ceres Dixon?" she said.

"Yes," Ladybelle responded for her.

"Room 11. First hallway to the right, first room on your left."

*

Marta held her arm tightly, reminding Ceres of the bruises she had sustained from Cane.

"I'm not going anywhere you don't tell me, Marta. You can let go," she pleaded.

"Take all your clothes off," Ladybelle said shutting the door to Room 11 behind them.

Ceres looked up at her, "Are you going to leave?" she asked.

"No."

"Can you turn around?"

"No."

"Can you not look at my body while I change?"

"Yes," she said.

She kept Ceres's eye contact the entire time as she unbuttoned her shirt, pulled off her blood-stained t-shirt and jeans, and stood there in her underwear and bra, holding her shirt and jeans in her hands. She remembered the seeds were in her jean's pocket.

"I think you should leave," Ceres said.

"I can't," she replied. "It goes against protocol."

"I will stay," Marta said. "You make her uncomfortable."

"Figures," Ladybelle said back. "Put her clothes, all of them, in this," she said handing Marta a coarse blue bag. Then she left.

"Thanks," Ceres said.

"We are not friends. I will not let you get away with anything," she said staring at her.

"Are you getting off on this?"

Marta kept her head straight forward, sighed, and shut her eyes, "You have a few seconds."

Ceres quickly bent her knees, squatting to the floor, slipped the pouch of seeds from her jeans pocket and, with the flick of her wrist, slid them under the hospital bed.

She turned around and took off her bra and underwear, and covered herself in a hospital garment. "I'm ready," she said. Marta opened her eyes, collected the clothing, and left.

As Ladybelle waited for Marta to return with the clothes, Mort approached her, seemingly out of nowhere. “Room 12. Five minutes,” he growled. He turned again towards the elevator and pressed UP. He gave her a look she hadn’t seen often.

“You’re not going to wait?” she asked turning around.

Mort turned his head to the side before walking into the elevator. “I’ll see you up there.”

“Thanks,” she said under her breath. She looked to the side and snapped her finger at one of the plump nurses behind the counter. The shorter of the two wobbled over to the slender blonde. Ladybelle imitated a smile, “When she orders...”

The nurse nodded knowingly. She pulled out her notepad and pencil and Ladybelle grabbed it from her, scribbling down directions for her new guest.

The nurse merely looked at the pad and placed it back in her pocket.

Room 12 was on the top floor of the building. There were more than twelve rooms in the infirmary, but 12 was saved for special occasions, board meetings and celebrations.

Ladybelle made her way up to the top floor alone, using her frosted reflection in the elevator door to fix flyaways from her slicked back ponytail. She patted her head almost neurotically; smoothing her hair several times and inspecting, then several times more.

She pulled her white buttoned-up shirt down and rolled her shoulders back as the door beeped and opened.

"Ladybelle," an older man greeted her.

"Sir," she bowed her head, almost curtsied.

The man asked her to sit, with his hand held out to the side, gesturing to a long oval table. She raised her eyes to its gleaming cherry oak surface. Mort was sitting already, clicking the same pen he used to sign contracts in the days before. Next to him was Mae, in public relations. The only other person in the room was the bookkeeper, Donna, who sat expectantly with her typewriter.

"We'll begin," the man said.

Ladybelle knew that this was no celebration. Donna typed the first two words the man said, and everything else clicked onto the paper.

Ladybelle sat quietly on the opposite side of the table from Mort and Mae. She made eye contact with Mort briefly before turning her gaze to Mae.

"Mae, why are we meeting today?" the old man asked, sitting down at the head of the table.

Mae took the side of her glasses and placed them back up the bridge of her nose. "The murder," she said calmly. Ladybelle's stomach dropped.

"Oh, alright. We'll get to that," click, click, click. "Before that, what are the current numbers?"

Mae shuffled the papers in front of her. Ladybelle and Mort knew that this was only a formality. He already knew the numbers; he was just drawing out the inevitable.

"Consumer trust is up 3% since this week's 14% drop. Sales have risen 25% since our last campaign. We are at 86% contract renewal with growers and nine of ten college students support funding for science related studies on genetic modification." She lowered her papers, "The last is neither here nor there presently. We need to follow up to enquire if they want studies to further modification or to prove that it is bad. Either way, we have donations from them and willing participants."

The man looked at Donna and she stopped typing the last of Mae's statement.

The man signaled Donna to leave and she packed up her typewriter carefully and quickly, clicking her heels on the floor as she left like her fingers on the keyboard.

The man watched her leave; he watched the door shut quietly.

"Mae, can you tell us what our numbers would look like if it was revealed that we murdered a child?"

Mae turned her head towards Ladybelle. "Consumer trust in products would likely decline after consumer trust in The Foundation decreased. In the past, accidental, or even intentional deaths, due to Foundation employees, or even Foundation employees themselves, has decreased sales and profitability by roughly 20%." She looked up at the man and he signaled for her to continue. "This would lead to eventual loss of contracts, which would lead to loss of capital, loss of funding in the labs, loss of the best graduates, loss of the business. It's a slippery slope." She smiled demurely at the man and he nodded in approval.

There was silence in the conference room. Mort clicked his pen once more, breaking the silence before returning it back to his jacket pocket.

Ladybelle felt the pressure of the air in the room. She clenched her teeth and breathed in heavily. "The victim had already seen too much," she finally said. "That is more of a liability than what we did."

The man nodded his head in understanding. "Now, Ladybelle," he said holding his hands together, pushing his knuckles into the opposite palm, alternating sides. "We don't just go around killing— even if they are on the wrong side. We imprison, we rehabilitate. We bring them in. Soldiers are soldiers regardless of what they've seen. Soldiers are amplified because of what they've seen. You should know that, Ladybelle."

There was silence again.

"What if someone would have arbitrarily killed you?" he finished.

She looked across the table at Mort, then stared quietly down at the table, the grain appearing as darkened life lines in the cherry oak.

"Everyone has a use," he continued. "Ceres is perfect—she has no one to live for. Perhaps she'll live for the purpose we give her, and she's young. For now, Ladybelle will be retrained. Mort will sign the remainder of the contracts alone. Mae, you will find out what we need from the girl." He looked around at all of the faces at the table. "We're done for today."

The man left first, leaving them to sit awkwardly until Mort stood up and followed behind him. Then, as Ladybelle walked out the door, she stopped Mae, holding her arm back. "Can't we just say that this was another casualty of the group wanting to blow up the Foundation? Why can't we just say that?"

She whispered under her breath, "Always creating more work, Ladybelle. I'm not here to just clean up your messes. If we kept publicizing that people want to blow up the Foundation, people will start to wonder if there is a good reason for wanting to destroy it." She pulled her arm away and turned down the hall.

Ceres pulled the curtain around the bed and sat on it. She pulled at the perfectly sewn edges of the gown. She leaned all the way back onto the waxy sheet of paper that was pulled out to protect clients from germs. She liked how clean it was. She remembered what clean was like. Sterile. There hadn't been anything this clean on the farm.

There was a knock at the door and a crackle of paper as Ceres quickly sat up. It was a young woman, a brunette. She reached forward to shake shook Ceres's hand.

"I'm Michelle," she said. She was pretty; her hair was down. Ceres did not shake her hand.

"You look pretty beat up. I bet you'd like a shower," she said.

"I'd like a private shower, yes," she replied.

"No problem. I'm not a huge fan of watching people shower anyway," she laughed.

Ceres felt comforted by her, comfortable enough to say, "Those people, they're horrible."

Michelle pushed her lips together, "They think you are horrible."

"What do you think?" she said back.

"I think that everything requires a little critical thought, and I never judge any circumstance by what it seems to be."

Ceres smiled. Michelle unlocked the door on the other side of the room to reveal a pristine bathroom with white walls and white shower curtain.

Michelle left Ceres alone in the bathroom. When the door closed, the latch made a noise that made her believe that she had been locked in. She checked and the door opened to reveal Michelle on the other side, waiting.

"You have a set of clothes in the cupboard in there," she said. "We will wash yours and give them back to you."

Ceres disappeared again behind the door.

She opened the cupboard to see sets of yellow cotton pants and white t-shirts. She shut the cupboard again and peeled the gown from her skin. She was happy to have something else to wear.

She turned on the shower and left the water running as she looked in the mirror at her naked body. She turned to look at her bruises from Cane, the slash on her face, the dye from her attempt to be someone else. She looked at the smeared mascara under her eye from her endeavor to make her makeup match her new hair color. She pulled in, close to the circular mirror that crimped out from the wall. She flipped it to the magnifying side and looked at the color of her eyes.

When she got out of the shower, she toweled off her hair to reveal a residue of black hair dye before wrapping the towel in a spiral and letting it sit on her head. She put on the t-shirt and pulled the drawstrings of the pants. Her nipples showed through the shirt; it embarrassed her. She put on a second shirt over the first.

When she unraveled her towel, her hair was considerably lighter. It was no longer black, but a dark brown. She considered the idea that she didn't purchase permanent hair color and she was happy.

She combed through her hair, thinking about her mother's brush and the jeweled engravings on the back side. She liked looking at the design seemingly float over the top of her hair like a crown. These brushes were clean, sterile, save for a single strand of white hair tied tightly around one of the spokes.

Ceres thought about what kind of person was imprisoned in Room 11 before, who else had been required to strip down and remove everything personal from themselves?

Spotting a blow dryer on the side of the sink, Ceres dried her hair on low, moving her head from side to side to get a better look at the legion on her face. There was a soft knock on the door.

"Yes?" she said turning the dryer off.

"Are you finished? I'd like to begin my exam," the woman said.

"Yes," though she was not; but Michelle had been the most normal person she had encountered and she didn't want to make it uncomfortable between them.

She opened the door to Michelle's smile, "Sit on the table please."

Ceres did.

Michelle started with her vitals. She gave a quick smile and asked for the usual "deep breath."

"Do you know about my friends?"

"Yes," she responded without elaborating.

"Can you tell me?"

"No," she added. She stopped and looked up at the glass partitions to the hallway, "officially I cannot comment on your two friends who are in the West Hospital."

Ceres felt her stomach drop. "Can you unofficially tell me which two friends you are speaking of?"

Michelle stopped again and looked her directly in the eyes, "I can tell you that two people are alive that came in with you, a third is not."

Ceres knew that Bry and Alta were alive, Sege had died in the doorway, or at the door, wherever or however far he had gotten before the shot was heard that sent them running from his cabin. She wished it were Bry and Sege. Then she felt anger at herself for wishing that someone were dead.

"What is going to happen to me here? Are you going to put some drugs in my IV that sedate me until I'm not a real person anymore? Can you just tell me now so I can hang myself with the curtains?"

Michelle laughed a little, "Ceres, you can't hang yourself with the curtains, because you can't get them off the walls. They go into the floor, they are taut enough that it would be impossible for you to wrap them around your neck."

Ceres stared at the door, "I won't take an IV. No life is better than a life in a stupor."

"I think there are many people that would beg to differ with you, Ceres. I will not put you on an IV, although I think you might need one."

Ceres thought about it further, "Just fluids? Like the things that help with dehydration? I'll be okay with that. No medicine. No chemicals."

"Chemicals are good for you, sometimes. I'll order you one with just the saline. You'll feel better. I will, however, need to give you some kind of medicine for that cut," she said pointing at Ceres's cheek.

"She would have killed me," she blurted.

"Looks like it, with a rusty knife, too!" Michelle replied.

"No," Ceres replied in disbelief.

"It's a saying," she laughed.

"No it's not. I've never heard it."

"Just because you've never heard it doesn't mean that it doesn't exist."

Ceres bore the rest of the examination in silence, inspecting the dimly lit room. Michelle stitched up Ceres's wound and asked about her bruises; she said they were a result of the Occa's attack in the field. She didn't see any good in drawing Cane into an already convoluted problem.

"There'll be someone in to ask you if you want anything. Request anything. They will give it to you."

She left, and Ceres laid down.

A woman dressed in white and grey came into the room only moments later.

"May I get you anything, ma'am?" she asked.

"I don't know what to ask for," Ceres replied.

"I'll give you the lunch menu," she said.

Ceres looked over the menu.

The card listed various entrees; there was a turkey sandwich on soy crunch bread, a cranberry soufflé with turkey chunks which sounded unappetizing, a blue cheese crumble over iceberg lettuce, among various other strange food choices. Ceres decided on a cheese pizza; if it were to be her last meal, she would enjoy it.

"Anything from the other side?" the lady asked. Ceres flipped the menu over to the back side. It was a menu called *Comforts of Home.* Her eyes perused the items. There were warm socks; mittens; stuffed animals; knit blankets; pictures of animals: baby, jungle, forest; the Koran; a Bible; the Book of Mormon; books by Sylvia Plath, Mark Twain and curiously enough, *The Phantom Tollbooth.*

"A Bible. *The Phantom Tollbooth.* A toothbrush," she looked up, "is there a limit to these?" she asked.

The lady shook her head.

"One of each," she replied, handing her back the menu.

"You want every item?"

"Is it complementary?" she asked.

"Yes, dear."

"Then yes, please. I'll take one item of each. A pair of socks though," she laughed. "Wouldn't be much good with only one sock!"

The lady awkwardly smiled back at her. Ceres knew the words were not her own as they came out of her mouth. Bry had awkwardly spoken through her.

"Anything to drink?" the lady asked.

Ceres thought for a moment. "Water."

When the lady left, Ceres pulled the curtain and dove under the bed, searching for the seeds. She found them lodged in the corner underneath the wheel of the examination bed. She pulled at them as there was a knock at the door and it startled her. She moved the pack into the pocket of her pants and stood up.

"Everything alright?" Michelle asked.

"Yes. I thought I dropped something."

"What?"

"I thought I had a list in the pocket of my jeans. I was hoping that it would have fallen underneath the bed, but it didn't."

"What's on the list?" she asked.

"A list of Bible verses. The lady is going to bring me one, a Bible, and I wanted to look up the verses."

Michelle squinted her eyes. "Well, I can have the laundry check the pockets of your jeans for you. I don't really see any harm in letting you have Bible verses." Michelle knew they'd be checking the pockets anyway.

Ceres smiled at her and kept smiling. Michelle was caught off guard by it.

The doctor placed her IV after reassuring Ceres that it was simply saline.

"So, you'll hold onto this," she said indicating the metal pole that the saline bag was attached to, "and we'll walk to your room. Lisa has collected everything that you need and they'll bring your food there too."

"Is this so I can't run?" she said looking at the catheter in her hand.

"No, this is so you can live," Michelle responded. Ceres stood barefoot on the cold ground. She grasped the pole and followed as Michelle opened the door. The hallway was quieted by her presence. Everyone seemed to look over at her and she was happy that she had worn two shirts.

Ceres started to smile at everyone, not because she liked them; rather, she *wanted* to be happy. Her mother always told her to put a pencil in her teeth when she was upset, like Pollyanna. *It is hard to hate someone who is smiling at you*, she would say. These people seemed unphased by the smiling; their fear and hatred was apparent in the way they moved away from her in the hallway and their unfriendly glares.

"Michelle," she said. "I'd like a room with a view."

Michelle looked back at her and nodded. She then looked forward to press the UP button on the elevator.

Ceres hadn't noticed the two men in white scrubs that were acting as body guards as they were walking down the hall. She only became aware of them when they entered the elevator with her and Michelle. The men stood in front of the women with folded arms.

Suddenly, Ceres felt as if she were in a mental institution. She must be crazy. Considering what had happened in the last 72 hours, she felt that perhaps she was insane, and maybe needed to be drugged. There was no way she would recover from what had happened, to her, Sege, Bry. The death hadn't ended. It was only beginning.

The elevator doors opened to a green floor. Ceres thought it looked friendlier than the one she had just left. It appeared to be a hotel, not an infirmary. They took a turn to the left and walked to the end of the hall. Her room was the second to the last on the right with a golden C on the thick cherry oak door. When Michelle opened it, the room was yellow and orange, and quite cheerful.

"You'll be happy here," Michelle said.

"Happy," Ceres repeated.

Ceres looked around the room at the white-wood four poster bed and the yellow fuzzy carpet underneath her feet. She curled her toes in the rug's fibers. She had the feeling that she'd been in the room before; it was a feeling she couldn't place. She saw a dresser and an armoire, a bench and a table. "There isn't a view," Ceres noticed.

"It's best that you get your rest and don't focus on anything from the outside world," Michelle said.

Ceres eyes grew wider, "What am I supposed to focus on?"

Michelle motioned her to sit down at the table, which only had one chair.

"You'll be here until you are better. Then you will go somewhere else. I advise you to enjoy it here. You never know how good or bad the next place will be."

Michelle shut the door behind her and left Ceres alone. Ceres felt as if she was in a bedroom in an old familiar house. She sat at the table and stared at the shapes in the texture of the wall. She knew that they would force her to go mad here. They already thought she was a terrorist of some kind; they had killed her on national television, and there wasn't anything in her imagination that she could rule out.

She crossed her legs and fingered the entrance of the IV into the back of hand.

Knocks at the door alarmed her.

Lisa wobbled in with an entire plastic box of items for Ceres. She was followed by a tall boy in white scrubs who was carrying her pizza and bottled water.

He placed the food on the table; the box landed with an accidental clunk on the floor.

"Here you are, love," Lisa said kindly.

"Thank you," Ceres replied.

"We've put together some things for you to look at too. There's an album or two in here," she said tapping the lid of the box before standing up again.

"Thanks," Ceres said again.

"Buzz over there if you need anything else," indicating the telephone. "It only goes one place, so don't be fooled by the other buttons. There's a television hidden in the armoire but you'll only be able to watch the shows that are on the menu. If you get frustrated, don't try to break anything. They'll find a way to make you pay for it."

"I have nothing," Ceres said blankly.

"Those who have nothing still have means to pay," she said back. "Sleep tight."

The pair left the night.

Ceres voraciously ate the pizza, all the while thinking about what type of album she had been given. Her mouth began to feel dry as she couldn't produce enough saliva to keep up with the doughy crust of the pizza. She chugged the water then looked around to see if there was any other source of water in the room. When she saw that there wasn't, she slowed down.

When the pizza was finished, she pulled open the plastic box's top with a crack. She placed the lid on the table and started to pull out her new possessions. The first thing she did was place both socks on her now freezing feet. She rubbed her feet inside the socks and then rubbed them together on the floor.

Ceres stood up and decided to investigate each of the three doors in the room; the first door she had come in, the second, on the other side of the room next to her bed, and the third next to the table.

First she tried the knob of the door that she came in. It was locked, as she suspected. The door next to the table led to a shower and a sink. The door next to her bed led to a walk-in closet filled with clothes. Ceres picked up a pair of jeans, strangely, in her size. She flipped through the shirts, which were also in her size. She fell to the ground carefully as to not pull out the IV which was still in her hand, and looked at the tennis shoes, which were all in her size. She heard the door open in the main room and she quickly came out to see a lady leaving the room. On her bed were her clothes, pressed and clean with a note saying "Courtesy of the Foundation." Ceres picked them up and put them in the closet, making a place for them on the shelves that had various purses. She wondered why she would need a purse. They were trying hard to make it seem like home, but she hadn't needed a purse in months.

There was a door in the closet that was locked. That door concerned her greatly. When she left the closet, she locked it from the outside.

Ceres had always been afraid of closets.

She pulled out the album from the plastic box and sat quietly on the bed, cross-legged. She opened the black leather cover to reveal pictures of her dad and herself as a child. There were pictures of her mother and Aster, too. She flipped faster. Her cousin Erving. Her old house and her old room. Pictures of her nursery as a baby and her mother holding her. Then Ceres noticed her mother's ring in the picture and she turned it on her own finger—facing the pointed end of the heart towards the center of her knuckle. She smiled; it was the only thing she had left of her mother now that all of her belongings were lost to the Foundation. She looked closely at the picture and then around the room. The nursery looked identical to this room, she thought. The only difference was that the bed replaced her crib. She suddenly felt very tired. How had the Foundation been able to plumb her memories? And how would they use these memories to manipulate or control her? As if it were out of nowhere, her eyes heavied and she couldn't muster the strength to stand. Her feet were like logs and she thought for sure she had been drugged. She fell to the floor and her face found comfort on the shaggy pile of the carpet.

When she awoke, she was bed. Her whole body was snuggly under the covers save for her right hand, which was placed across her body. The IV catheter was still there, but stopped with a plastic cap. She pulled it out carefully, and held a tissue from the nightstand on it to absorb any blood.

She glanced around the room, with no concept of time. She didn't know if she'd been asleep for hours or minutes. Had she been tricked into sleeping her life away? She picked up the phone next to her bed and read the note that said, "One for Lisa."

She pressed the "one" and heard a ring.

"Lisa, dear."

"What time is it?" she asked, her voice a parched whimper.

"Two in the afternoon, love."

"How many days have I been here?" she asked.

"Just the one, dear."

Ceres heard the words, but there was no way to really tell how much time had passed. She didn't have a view of the outdoors to tell her what time it was. She didn't have the television news or a computer or a phone. She remembered the armoire and opened it, flipped to a channel then to the next before recognizing they were all essentially the same. She realized how dependent she was on the sun to tell her how to behave. She curled her feet up under her and sat up.

"Can I have a clock? And a window?" she asked softly.

"Yes and we'll see," she replied. "Anything else I can get for you this afternoon? Some food? Some wine? A soda?"

Ceres tried to remember when the IV had been removed and couldn't; she panicked. Then she reached into the pocket of her pajamas to feel for the burlap pouch. *Nothing.*

She heard static on the other end of the phone and then, "Is there a problem, dear?"

Ceres shook her head.

"Dear?"

"No. I don't need anything. Water. Just water." Ceres realized that it wasn't the time or the place to execute a hunger strike, but she couldn't risk being subject to losing another 24 hours. She hung up the phone and dove under the sheets of the bed, searching for the pouch. She was spiraling. She couldn't have lost something so important. She darted in and out of the starched sheets to no avail and finally decided to rip all of them off of the bed. She got up and threw off the white goose-down comforter onto the floor. Then, she pulled the sheet of the bed all the way back to see if the pouch had made its way into the hospital folded corners. Nothing. They were gone. She fell to her knees, searching under the bed. Nothing. She tried to remember if she had put them anywhere else. She couldn't remember. She couldn't remember anything she had done since she had been there. She didn't know where *there* was.

She could hear someone outside of her door. She pulled the sheets and comforter back onto a pile on the bed and stood waiting.

The door opened to reveal a red light, blinking somewhere above her door. The light reflected off of the back of the hallway wall. Two men in white scrubs walked in. One had her water, the other stood at the door.

Ceres looked at them expectantly. "Is there an issue?" she said.

"I was just about to ask you the same thing," the woman said, walking into the room. This wasn't anyone Ceres had seen before. She was older, maybe twice her age. She had brown hair that was short and well kempt. She wore a black pencil skirt and blazer, black high heels and stockings. She wore black-rimmed glasses and a barrette held the hair off of her face on the right side.

"You can leave," she said to the men in scrubs. "I'll buzz if she begins to get irate."

Ceres watched the men leave. "Sit," she said, "make yourself at home." She sat down on the bench along the wall. Ceres sat in the lone chair.

"Let's be very clear, here, Ceres. You are dead. Let's start with that. You died a few days ago. People rejoiced. We caught you and your friend, and now the world is safe again. You will not be leaving here, alive. You probably won't be leaving here dead, either."

Ceres, although displeased with the message, was happy with the lady's blunt nature.

"Thank you," she said. "That's the first real information anyone has given me."

"You are welcome," she said, "I'm Mae."

"Will you tell me something honestly, Mae?"

The woman nodded.

"Are my friends alright?"

Her eyes lit up. "Actually, that is exactly what I'm here for. One of your friends made us a deal," she said.

Ceres felt her stomach drop. She was sure it was Alta; that she had made some sort of twisted deal with the powers that be. She would have sold her soul to sell out Ceres. Her eyes stared a hole into the woman. She hardly blinked.

"You look terrified," she said. "It is a deal in your kindness." Ceres shook her head.

"I don't understand. What is the deal?"

"Your friend has sold himself for you."

"Sold *himself?*"

"He's signed the dotted line. He's entered into a partnership. He's contracted himself for the good of the world," Mae exaggerated her words with her hands.

"Bry would never do that. Even for me."

"Bry is on the other side of your bathroom right now in the adjoining room," she said flatly. "You didn't know that because we didn't want you to. You share a bathroom. He's quite nice. Not talking. But he seems nice. His silence has bought him a few more days here, but he should be careful. He won't be any good to us if he doesn't talk." She crossed her legs, "Let's talk about those seeds."

Ceres looked over at the bathroom door.

"Let me see him, please."

"Lovers? Friends? Which is it? He had a telling look on his face when we told him you had died in the transfer. He has quite the strong feelings for you. I suspect that is why he is not talking."

"What makes you think you can just toy with people like this? Who do you think you are?" She picked up the album. "How did you get all of these pictures?"

The woman leaned forward in her chair. "We're the people, Ceres. We have everything"

Ceres leaned over in likeness, "No, I'm the people. You're the Foundation."

The lady seemed tired of this business. "Your life has been bought for you. Sege has bought it."

"He's dead," Ceres said skeptically.

"No. If you've learned anything, you should have learned that *nothing* is as it seems. He travelled here with Bry. They think you're dead, you thought they were dead. Now you know the truth. We will keep you."

"What did he do for that? My life?"

"He agreed to join our research program at the university."

"He wouldn't," she whispered. Sege always talked about how their studies were fixed.

"He did. But Ceres, it doesn't come without a catch. You will live no matter what, so we can't use your life against you, but there is no contract for Bry. A life for a life was our deal."

"And how am I supposed to keep Bry alive?" she said defiantly.

"That is why I came to you. I want to know about the seeds."

Ceres stood up and sat down again.

"I'd like to get out of here," she said. "I will tell you anything you want to know, but can we take a walk?"

The lady stood and walked to the door. She buzzed herself out without a word to the girl. Ceres sat back down on the bed.

"Be ready in 10 minutes," she said. "And Ceres," she said looking at the table with the album, "think about your family."

Ceres quickly went into the closet and dressed in her own greyed t-shirt and jeans.

Ceres tucked in her aunt's necklace under her t-shirt and pulled her hair back into a pony tail. She laced her shoes and when she exited the closet, the door to the hallway was open. Mae stood waiting.

"I'm just going to use the restroom," she said.

"Be quick," was the reply.

Ceres did not need to use the restroom, but instead she went into the room and rummaged through the drawers. She found a drawer of makeup and scribbled "Bry, stay alive" on the cabinet under the sink with eye-liner. She stood and looked up and around without moving her head, trying to locate where they had placed the camera. She resolved to think that it was, perhaps, behind the mirror and hoped that Bry would see the note before it was removed by the establishment.

Ceres walked out of the room and into the hall.

The lady was not alone anymore. The two men in scrubs were back. They followed a few steps behind, waiting for Ceres to make a run for it, or to attack someone. They were told that she was dangerous to herself and to others, so they were nervous at her every move.

They headed down the hallway to the elevator, passing Ladybelle heading in the opposite direction. Ceres sneered. Mae ignored her. They went down to the first floor without speaking. The lady looked over at Ceres and smiled before the doors opened.

"On your best behavior, Ceres. You aren't invincible," Mae smiled.

The doors opened to reveal a large fountain. They were in the Foundry Park in the city; the same park that she and Aster's son Erving had played in as little kids.

"I know this place," she said softly.

"Yes, most children in the area have been here at one time or another. Most people don't realize that it is Foundation owned and operated."

Ceres breathed in the fresh air and closed her eyes. It smelled exactly like it used to when she was a child. It smelled like a memory: crisp air, apples, pine trees.

"Shall we walk around the fountain for a bit? Hopefully that will help your mind."

"Sure," she replied. The Foundry Park was large and triangular. The fountain was at the top of the triangle with a circular building smoothing out the edge of the sharp point at the top. The half circle building was several stories tall with silver edges and mirrored windows. The Foundation factories were behind, out of the triangle. That was where Sege was; where they worked on their poisons and genomes. There were cast iron gates, ten feet high, to the left and to the right—twenty yards away on each side.

"Won't someone recognize me?" she said to the lady curiously. "If I'm *dead*, won't they know I'm not?"

The lady laughed, "You're smart." She reached out and held Ceres's arm in hers as they walked. "We closed this park to the public two years ago, your junior year of high school, I believe. Everyone here is in the employ of the Foundation. They all know about you. There was a memo. That's why people are looking at you strangely." Ceres didn't find it very funny. "Down at the bottom of the triangle, a ways down, are the gardens now, the greenhouses. They are encased in ten foot ivory walls. The city wasn't very happy at first but we threw some money their way and they built another park on the other side by the school, Atkins. You surely must know it; it was there when you went there."

Ceres thought back to another lifetime and remembered when they erected a fountain by her school, how Sege had said something about "the Man" then, but she didn't pay much attention to it.

"Money buys you a lot," Ceres said meanly.

"Yes, Ceres. Money buys you everything," Mae replied patting her hand. "Let's sit on this bench and you can tell me about the seeds."

Ceres sat down. "I don't know what you want to know."

"Let's start with where you got them."

"I don't know," she lied.

"Don't be coy with me. We're friends. Who gave them to you?" she said.

"Just someone I knew."

"Are there more?" she said looking at her sidelong.

"I don't know. I didn't even know what they were until Sege."

"And what are they?"

Ceres smiled, "They're Heirloom."

"No. No they aren't," Mae said smugly.

"Yes, Sege tested them and they are Heirloom."

The lady looked up at one of the men in white scrubs and he turned and made his way back to the building.

"Perfect," she said.

Ceres panicked, "Didn't you know that? I thought that was why you were after us?"

"Yes, of course we knew that."

Ceres knew that she had told a secret that she shouldn't have and she didn't know how to correct it. She didn't know that Sege had told the Foundation that he had created the signal himself, that there were no such heirloom seeds, instead only imposters that he had fabricated. That he did it to mess with them, give them a little chase.

"Can I see Bry?" Ceres asked again.

"Yes. You'll see him soon."

"Alive?"

The lady patted Ceres's leg and stood up, "Yes, unless he does something that he shouldn't. Then I suspect he will come to an untimely end."

"Can I see Sege?" she asked, knowing the answer.

"No. That was part of the agreement. He can see you, but you cannot see him. Perhaps you can take comfort in that information." Ceres snarled her lip and shook her head. "Well we can't have everything," the lady replied.

As they got up to go inside, Ceres stopped at a large white sculpture that was new to the fountain. It was of a man, short, portly and pointing to the sky off in the distance. He had a book in his hand with a cross on it that Ceres assumed was a Bible. Inscribed on the floor was a plaque that read: Proverbs 11:26 "The people curse him who holds back grain, but a blessing is on the head of him who sells it." She felt as if she had read it before, maybe in Aster's verses.

"Who is that?" she asked.

"That's Prom Dierts, he's the founder of the Foundation," she laughed at the repetition. "He is the one that created all of this," she said, "from nothing. He is the American Dream. A real hero. A scientist that saved plants from extinction." She sounded as if she was reading from a guidebook. "He was a poor grower's son who lost everything to the drought of '73. His mother abandoned him and his father, so he pulled himself up by his bootstraps and figured out how to save his father's farm, so that his mother would come back."

"Did she?" Ceres said raising an eyebrow.

"No. She didn't. She was nowhere to be found. Ever. He searched for her endlessly until he thought for sure she was dead. When he first started his business, he went from door to door, selling his creations. Giving farmers a chance against any future droughts or bad seasons. He's a saint. Would you like to meet him?"

Ceres shrugged her shoulders. She didn't know what she would say to a man that had created the epidemic.

"You can if you give up the seeds' location," Mae taunted.

Ceres smiled and walked back to the doors. She really didn't know where the seeds were. She knew they were somewhere in her room, at least she hoped that was where they were.

She thought of how Bry's story was similar to Prom's. She wondered if it was worse to have your mother leave or die.

Ceres returned to her room with her guard in tow, eager to see if Bry had seen her message and if he had written anything back.

The guard stopped at the door and made sure that it shut with Ceres on the other side. Ceres watched the door shut as well, and then ran to the restroom to inspect the message. The door was locked. Ceres pulled at the door and it wouldn't budge. She banged on it and then remembered the red light in the hallway and calmed down. She sat back, a few feet from the door and inspected it. She noticed an illuminated placard on the right side of the door. She stood up to see that it said, "Occupied." She wondered how she hadn't seen it before.

"Bry," she whispered. She sat with her back on the door and elbowed the door quietly. "Bry," she said again. She could hear water running and she waited for it to stop before saying his name again.

She felt the door move slightly. "Bry," she said louder.

Bry put his head up to the door and listened carefully while he dried his hands.

"Bry," the voice said again.

"Ceres?" he responded.

"Bry, it's me!" she whispered loudly.

Ceres started to cry and then tried to stop herself. "Bry are you okay?"

"Ceres, they said you *died.*"

"I wrote you a note on the cabinet."

"I don't see it," he said.

Ceres knew that that meant there wasn't much time.

"We have to get out of here."

Bry quieted on the other side, "We won't get out of here, Ceres."

"We have to try, Bry. We have to try."

The door opened to the bathroom and Bry was taken by two of the scrubbed men. A like group of men stormed into Ceres's room and pulled her from the floor.

They met face-to-face in the hallway. The guards held Ceres under her arms. Her body was unable to find its footing underneath her. Bry's hands were held together behind him and he was pushed by the strongest of the men in white scrubs.

"You want to be together so badly, we will put you together," Mae said angrily and holding up the pouch that the seeds had been in. It was empty now.

Ceres lost all of the air in her lungs.

They both knew that nothing good could come of this change. Bry's right eye was swollen shut and he had a wound on his right arm that ran up the length of his forearm to the middle of his bicep. Ceres didn't know when he had sustained the injury and figured it must have been when she had left him in the field by the cabin. His shirt had a faint stain of blood from her run-in with Alta.

They were led to the service elevator on the other side of the hall and pushed to the back wall. They faced their reflections on the frosted silver wall and no one spoke. Mae accompanied them down. Ceres felt the pit of her stomach turn over again with the speed of the elevator. She closed her eyes and moved forward.

"What's wrong, girl?" the man holding her right side hissed. "This is only the beginning of your discomfort."

Ceres shot him a look, "Your suffering will always be more than mine." The man laughed at her response and the elevator stopped.

They were taken down a hollow corridor with aluminum bolted panels.

"Wondering about the sudden change of scenery?" Mae snapped. She didn't wait for a response. "They found your seeds during our little chat and we are cultivating them. We believe that you don't know if there are any more or not, so your use to us has diminished." She stopped at a steel reinforced door and scanned her name badge on it. She looked back at Ceres, "We said that you wouldn't die, but we didn't say we would make it comfortable for you."

They entered through the door to reveal a hodgepodge of misfits and hooligans.

"Welcome home," she said. "You'll be quite miserable here."

The door shut behind them and locked. Ceres fell into Bry. He held her head uncomfortably with his left arm, unable to bend his right without wincing. She breathed into his shirt, smelling an unfamiliar smell; they had taken his things as well. "How could she know all of that in only minutes?" Ceres said into his shirt, but he couldn't understand it.

After a short minute, Ceres opened her eyes to the others in the room. It was an underground barrack, filled with bunk beds with grey sheets. There were various others there, wearing the same kinds of white or grey t-shirts and blue jeans. They didn't look like they weren't cared for. They were clean. They wore shoes. They looked like they had eaten.

Ceres pulled away from Bry and walked towards the one standing in the middle of the room, waiting to greet their new roommates.

"Hello," Ceres said. "I'm Ceres. This is Bry."

"Rep," he said in a rasp that reminded her of Aster.

Ceres felt the awkwardness of the room. "We're leaving tomorrow," Rep said quietly. "We've been planning this for weeks."

"How?" Bry said.

"Never mind how," he snapped, "Do you want to stay or do you want to leave?"

Bry thought that Rep must've been crazy. His hair was a mess of grey and black wires. His face was smooth, like it was young, but his forehead told a story of many years of life.

"I'm leaving with them," Ceres said. She turned to Bry, "You are coming too."

"You'll be last out," Rep said. "It's only fair."

Bry stared at her. "Wait a minute, Ceres. What kind of crack plan are you going to fall into? Do you really want to risk your life?"

Ceres looked at him squarely, "You said yourself you have to live in order to die. I won't die here. They may have what they want but they won't have me too."

Their dinner was delivered at exactly 6 PM. They ate at a picnic table at the back of the room. There were six of them together who were planning to leave, of the ten in the room when they'd arrived. They had sat at separate tables. The four that weren't planning on leaving were mostly older, happy to be taken care of in a place with a bed and a warm meal even if only for a night.

Ceres didn't want to ask where these people were from, or who they were. She didn't want to develop any type of attachment to any of them. Bry kept trying to caution her silently. His looks began to annoy her, so she placed herself so that his face was out of her view.

"How?" Ceres finally asked, breaking the silence of the table.

"There was a note, today, telling us how to escape and when, and there was a key," another of the group said.

"How do you know it can be trusted?" Bry asked.

Rep put his spoon down and stared at him. "We don't," he said.

"Seems pretty stupid to trust a note from inside these walls," Bry commented with a laugh.

"It's the only hope we have," a lady said.

"It seems like it's from a legitimate source, Ceres," Rep said. "There is a small vent hidden behind that stove. It was locked but the key they sent unlocks it," he said pointing at the small kitchenette. "The stove doesn't work, it's just for show."

Even though he had addressed her concern for the heat from the stove, she couldn't help but imagine crawling down the vent into the pits of hell.

"Where does it lead?" Ceres asked.

Rep leaned in closer, "to the outside."

"Why would they do that?" Bry said. "Why would they put their prisoners in a place that had a direct path to the outside? That's just stupid."

"You are in or you're out. We don't care either way," he said leaning back on his tailbone. "You have until 8 AM to decide."

"Where will you go? When you are out?" Ceres asked.

"To safety," he replied.

Ceres rolled her eyes to the side. "Can you be more specific? Is anywhere really safe?"

Rep looked around. He was so obviously skeptical of everything around him. He was more of a conspiracy theorist than Sege ever was. "Epineio. It is safety."

Ceres started to question Rep's sanity, but seeing as though he presented the only option for escape, she decided that she would take her chances.

Ceres and Bry were the last one's left sitting at the table. Rep and his buddies had taken their spots, leaving two beds on opposite sides of the room.

"Sege talked about that place," Bry said quietly. "In the van, he whispered it to me when they were distracted with Alta."

"What happened to her?" she asked.

"She went insane. She tried to come on to one of the Occa in the back of the van. She said that she didn't want anything to do with us, or you. That we were nothing to her. She said that she was switching sides and she didn't have any loyalty to you. Then they tased her and she died."

Ceres's eyes widened even bigger as the story went on. It sounded like her escape plan for a similar situation. "I didn't know you could die from being tased."

"They thought it was funny. They were laughing at her body on the bed of the van. Then they kept her there, dead. Sege just looked forward after he told me. He didn't look at her face. It was if she was looking directly at him the whole time. I just looked for a second, and I can still see it in my head now," he paused, "I wouldn't wish that on anyone. Listen, Sege said to go to Epineio if we ever got out, but I don't think it's guaranteed safety."

Ceres got up and left Bry at the table.

They started off on either side of the room from one another. Ceres lay in her bed and stared at the brick wall. She pulled the blanket all the way up under her chin and then pulled her blanket off again.

She walked over to the bookshelf by the table and looked at the books. There were many that she had had in her collection before her parents died. There were some that she saw in the corners of the farmhouse. One that she had had in her plastic box upstairs in her bright room. She pulled each book out and slid them back in quietly. She slid out *The Bell Jar* and fingered through the pages. She smiled, remembering how she hated the ending and wished she could have rewritten it. Finally, she found the Bible and retreated with it to the table.

She retrieved the list of verses that had been washed in the small pocket of her jeans. The ink was smudged and the paper was thin but she was still able to find every verse.

When she crawled into bed, it was Bry's. He was lying on his unwounded side. She held the Bible between them and lifted his arm, placing it around her.

"What's this?" he said, "Reminding me that someone's watching? *Don't make a move, Bry,*" he said in a deep voice not his own.

"The kingdom of heaven is like a mustard seed, which a man took and planted in his field. It is the smallest of *all* seeds, but when it grows, it is the biggest of the plants and becomes a tree, and the birds come and perch in its branches," she whispered.

She pulled away from him a little, "It was Aster's last verse."

"Are you the mustard seed?" he said sleepily.

She nestled her head against his chest and his stomach rumbled.

"You didn't eat," she murmured. "You have to eat to live," she said, mocking what he had said on the farm. He chuckled a little before falling fast asleep.

The next morning, at 7:45 AM, Rep and his followers were up and collecting themselves in the kitchen area. They sat at the table and waited. Ceres and Bry were up and standing next to them.

"I will go first," Rep said. "Then Dorna, Sam, Lista, Horrace and Bard." Then he looked at the couple, "Then you two will go last and pull back the stove and shut the vent. Think you can handle that?"

Bry nodded, "Yes, sir." It was obvious that he didn't want to go, and was only complying for Ceres's sake.

Rep looked at the clock and waited until there was one minute until 8 AM, as if the key would only work at that very time. He got up and moved the stove to reveal the vent and the entrance to the outside. It was large enough for a grown man to squeeze through it.

"Y'all are stupid for going down that hole," one of the naysayers said. She was sitting up in her bed and looking over at them. "That's not going to take you home," she continued.

"Neither is laying in that bed, Nabei," he retorted and popped off the vent. Nabei was a younger Asian woman, part of a foursome of two older women and one old man. Ceres thought that maybe she was staying because the others wouldn't make the crawl to the outside.

Nabei watched them as Rep waited for the clock to strike. Then he went in first, as he had outlined. They could hear clangs under their feet for a minute, then nothing. Moments later, Dorna followed with the same clangs, then Sam, Lista, Horrace and finally Bard. When it was time to go, Nabei picked up her refrain again.

"Don't," she said to Ceres and Bry.

They turned around to her. "Come too," Ceres pleaded.

"It's not safe," she said back. "Here you are alive. There you are underground."

Ceres looked back at the vent and then at Bry.

"I'll go first," he said.

They heard a few clangs again. Then they increased rapidly with a rumble. Ceres went over to the kitchen, far enough away to see a corner of the entrance. The clangs were coming back up from the vent and then there was a greased swirl of flames that pushed out of it and roared quietly into the room. The kitchen was on fire and Rep was gone. Bry pushed Ceres back into the table and pushed the stove back into the hole in the wall. It quickly erupted in flames and the red lights started to flash in circles on the walls.

There was a whistle and the sprinklers sputtered on, quenching the fire and drenching Ceres and Bry, Nabei and the three others. Nabei didn't move from her bed, even in the fire; she stayed sitting up and facing the kitchen. The others were awake now, too, staring at the pair.

When the fire was quenched, Ceres started laughing in response to the terror. Bry started laughing at her laughter and they began to dance around in circles under the sprinklers.

"Your bangs look so stupid wet!" he laughed.

"Your face is stupid wet or dry," she responded. They were crazy. They looked as if they were possessed. Nabei watched as they danced and insulted one another.

Suddenly, Ceres couldn't see anything but the imagined charred bodies trapped and twisted in the vent and she stopped dancing.

"Stop," she said as Bry held her hands and splashed in the water with his feet. "Stop!" she yelled and pushed him. He stopped abruptly and furrowed his brow at her, confused.

"They're all dead. All of them, and we were supposed to be in there, dead, with them, not dancing around like, like..." she pointed at the ground beneath her.

"We're not, Ceres. We're not dead. We're still here," he said back. "There is nothing wrong with celebrating making the right decision."

Ceres felt as if there was something wrong with reveling in her right decision when others had made the wrong one just moments earlier and paid with their lives.

She moved out of the direct spray of the sprinklers and leaned against the wall.

Bry walked over to Nabei and towered over her, still sitting in her bed.

"Where is the note?" he demanded.

"I didn't receive the note. It was not for me," she answered stoically.

"Did you read it? When did it get here? Why wasn't it for you?"

He pointed his finger at her as he spoke. She peeled the sheets back on the bed and stood up next to him. She could look him directly in the eye. She was tall and strong; she was not someone that Ceres would have wanted to stand up to.

"There are things that you do not know," she said firmly.

"No shit, lady. There's a whole crapload of things that I don't know. That's why I'm askin'," he said, wiping the water from his face.

"Maybe instead of probing me about the note, you should be thanking me for saving your lives," she said intensely over the sirens in the room.

Ceres moved from the wall momentarily to thank her, until Bry started speaking again and stopped her from joining.

"You didn't *do* anything. You just…" he continued until he was interrupted by the older man in the room.

"We're on the same side, guy" he said, holding his palm against Bry's wet chest.

"You don't know that," Bry said pushing his arm down.

"You wouldn't be in here if we weren't," he replied.

The alarms stopped, leaving his last word loud and echoing in the room.

The door opened and a crew of five or so workers were led in to clean up the room. A familiar face, Marta, led them, giving directions in her native language.

She found Ceres's eyes and said, "You and your friend will come with me."

When they left the room, Marta left it unlocked behind them. She was the only one there. She had not brought any of the other Occa. She wore her uniform, but did not wear her helmet. They exited down the hallway in a different way than they had come in.

The hall was long. It was longer than any hall that she had seen. After they had walked the corridor for about five minutes, Ceres started to notice that Marta was not enforcing them as much as guiding them. As Marta walked down the hallway, she held out a device to each of the surveillance cameras, presumably to temporarily disengage them.

At the end of the hall there was a door and the door led to six stairs. Marta told Ceres to open it. When she did, the light streamed in from the outside.

"Where are we going?" she said.

"You will go to the garden. I will go back," she replied.

Ceres looked confused and Bry looked skeptical as if it were another trick. The alarms still circled in the hallway.

"Go quickly. The door on the other side of the garden, through the terrarium, is not activated, but it will be," she said.

Bry headed out the door, but Ceres stayed for a moment. "Why are you doing this?" she asked.

Marta hesitated, "You are already dead. You went down the rabbit hole. I did not see you."

Ceres smiled again, backing away.

"Ten minutes," she said. "Only ten."

Ceres moved into the garden from the door. They were in a self-contained greenhouse garden with rows and rows of green stalks and plants. Ceres looked up the ivory walls and realized how far away they'd come from the Foundation building. They were in the area of the greenhouse with the tomatoes, ripe and red, bulbous and juicy. They looked amazing. Ceres knew she shouldn't eat anything. She didn't know what kinds of experiments they were doing with these plants.

"Bry, wait!" she whispered loudly. She searched for Bry and saw a figure in another, smaller greenhouse on the other side of the garden. She stepped through the rows of wooden planters and emerald leaves to the other side of the dome, then inside to see Bry standing over the blue corn and the door they were to go through on the other side, just yards away.

"Ceres," she heard a man say. She started to feel light headed— like the air had somehow changed.

She looked over at the man in the corner. He was old, dressed in khaki pants and a green plaid shirt.

"What's going on here?" she said, "Bry, we have to go."

Bry turned around to her. He looked like he was in a trance, and he was eating the blue and green corn that he had just picked off of the stalk. "I wanted to see what they were going to kill us for. This guy said it was okay to try it."

"Bry, no," she said taking it out of his hand. She didn't know how he could have been so misguided in the short time she had been with Marta at the end of the tunnel.

"What's wrong, little one? I told him it's okay," the man in the corner said. "It's just a little corn."

"It came from the earth, Ceres. It can't be that bad."

Ceres smiled a little, remembering how wrongly terrified she was of Bry the night by the river. She looked at him more closely. She knew his face. The cloudiness of her mind began to grow.

"Bry, we only have a few minutes," she said again.

"You're so young!" the man said, "You have your whole lives ahead of you."

"I'm sorry," she said, "Who are you?"

"Prom," he said standing up. She stood back from him. It was only then she noticed the puff of his oxygen tank, the tubes supplying fresh air to his nostrils.

"How did you do this?" she said, pointing at the corn. "These were seeds yesterday." Her speech was slowed in her mind and her words couldn't catch up to her brain. "What is this room?"

Prom simply smiled, "I can do a great many things."

"This seems like a better asset to your clients than spray," she sneered. "Bry, let's go," she said again. But this time, Bry didn't hear her; he had tumbled to the ground next to the planter. "Bry!" she screamed as she went to his aid.

"He will probably die," Prom said in a feeble voice, sitting in the corner of the domed greenhouse.

"Why did you let him eat that if you knew that it would kill him?"

"See what would have happened if you were to get your way and grow this on your own?" he said, with a snicker. "You would terrorize the country with your *heirloom* seed. You think you are doing something good, but you don't know anything."

Ceres looked at Bry's eyes as they glazed over with tears and she pushed on his stomach. "I'm sorry Bry," she said, "I'm so sorry." She looked up at the door Marta had indicated, only fifteen feet away.

"Ceres," Bry said, "I just want to go home. It wasn't so bad. Do you think there is any chance they'll let us go home?"

A tear rolled down her face and onto his. "Get up," she said, "Let's go home. We can go now."

Bry shook his head. "You need to leave me; you can go now. I'll meet you there," and closed his eyes, leaning his head over to her palm, cupping his face and nuzzling in it.

Ceres looked up at the door on the other side of the greenhouse and looked back to where Prom was no longer sitting.

She tried to lift his body, but couldn't budge him. She thought that she should stay with him, but she realized that it would be senseless for her to stay. She knew if she didn't get out of the room now, the air in the room would swallow her up. She leaned down to his cheek and kissed where her tear had fallen and moved backwards to admire his sweet face, imprinting it into her mind for the last time. She felt the air in the room fill her head— She wouldn't have long to make a decision.

Somehow it was so hard to decide— part of her wanted to try the corn too, a part of her wanted to sit and stay.

When she got up, her legs creaked as she stepped towards the door. Prom was nowhere to be seen. She looked back at Bry one last time and pushed open the door in the ivory wall. It opened easily, as if it had never been locked before and it closed loudly behind her. She was on the other side of the wall. She tried the door to come back in, but it was locked.

The outside world looked as if nothing had ever happened. She stood on the sidewalk next to the wall and looked both ways before stepping off of it and walking across the street. She didn't know if anyone was after her now, but she knew that they would be as soon as they found out she wasn't in the vent under the Foundation. She looked back at the wall again and could see the top of the enclosed greenhouse peak over the wall. To her right she saw the Foundation's factories, small in the distance.

When a loud siren rang, Ceres knew that she had been found out, except everyone on the street went into the building that they were next to in a panic. Ceres followed suit into an antique bookstore. She was the last one in before they locked the doors, leaving several people running up and down the street trying doors, banging on the glass, to see where they could find a safe haven.

She stood at the window of the bookstore looking out at the ivory walls and then she heard a faint explosion that got louder as the sound carried. She couldn't tell where it was from, and then she heard a second and a third. She placed her hand on the glass before the person next to her pushed her to the ground and the windows of the bookstore blew in with the pressure.

The man who pushed her down, his body was lying halfway on top of her. He had his face to the back of her neck, breathing heavily into her hair. The sirens were louder now and cries could be heard from all over the city. There was a cacophony of screams that she found disarming. She struggled to get up.

"Stay down," the man said. "Just for a minute more."

She did as he said, as if they were waiting for another blast that would never come. When others started to get up, she pushed away from him and stood up. Looking out the broken glass, she saw what had exploded; the Foundation was no longer on the horizon to her right. The only thing that she could see was the reinforced wall, unabated through the blast. The man ripped a strip of fabric from his shirt and tied it around his face, covering his nostrils. Ceres looked around for something to do the same. Before she could, the man ripped off another piece of his shirt and handed it to her, allowing her to tie it on herself.

He stepped up over the broken glass and through the window and ran across the street, pulling at the door that she had just exited from.

Ceres followed him.

"Get out of here," he said. "It's only a matter of time before the cloud."

"I came out of that door," she yelled through the screams. The citizens were running in the streets, cars trying to push through their herds.

"Prisoner or employee?" the man asked.

Ceres hesitated, "Prisoner."

"Alone?" he said.

She took a breath, "yes."

More cries, more sirens. "Rep? Nabei? Where are they?"

"Dead. Rep's dead. Nabei? I don't..." she stopped at the look on his face. "We need to go," she said pulling him along the sidewalk.

She wanted to ask where they should go. She wanted to ask who he was, or if he was the one to send the note, but she didn't. She was done asking questions. Whenever she asked questions, she was never satisfied with the answers.

He took the lead after the first street. He pulled her over people, through people, across debris and around cars jammed in the intersections; then he seemed as if he had no idea where he was going. He looked as if he was lost, unguided. He scratched his head, and wiped his brow.

"This way," he said, looking behind him to see the toxic plume over the Foundation's remnants. Ceres turned to see the unfamiliar skyline. "We don't have enough time to get out of the city," he said.

They went down an alleyway and down the stairs to the entrance of what appeared to Ceres to be a night-club. The man bashed on the door twice and then a third and fourth time. Ceres thought it was some sort of secret knock and didn't know what she had gotten herself into. Her eyes started to burn and she could smell the explosion through the ripped shirt. It smelled like Bry after he came in from spraying the fields. She started to feel the effects of the noxious odor on her body when the door finally opened.

u u u

As they walked into the dimly lit nightclub, she wanted to throw up, but she didn't want to show weakness to people she didn't know. She suppressed it for a moment until the saliva increased in her mouth and she could no longer keep it in. The door slammed behind her. She pulled off covering from her nose and fell to the ground, vomiting directly on the floor. It was nothing—stomach bile, water. It hurt to throw up, but it was the only thing her body was going to let her do.

The man who rescued her and another two men took off their over shirts and jackets and jammed them in the opening under the door. Ceres felt the lumps of stomach bile move up her esophagus and out onto the floor. She looked up from the ground and wiped her mouth when she saw a woman holding out water for her.

"I'm sorry, that's so disgusting," Ceres apologized.

"Don't worry about it. I'm sure worse things have happened on this floor," she winked at her.

Ceres's mouth moved slightly but not into a full smile. "I'm so embarrassed."

"We'll probably have the same reaction to the chemicals when we leave here," she said, winking again. It made Ceres uncomfortable that she had winked at her so many times in the short span of their conversation. It may have been a tick, a nervous one. Ceres always wondered if she had one that snuck past her observance, but it was only her sweaty palms that gave away her nerves.

The men stood in front of the door and spoke to each other in soft voices. The man who saved her began to get more animated, raising his hands, furrowing his brow. Then his hands moved to his waist. Ceres was sure that the man was informing them that their friends hadn't made it. She felt compelled to enter the conversation, so she brazenly walked up to them.

They stopped speaking. They stared at her.

The man in the middle lowered his gaze and said, "Can I assist you?"

"I thought I could tell you what I know," she said.

The man in the middle put his hand on the shoulder of the man who saved her, "Jack told us what we need, thanks." He dismissed her by ignoring her.

She nodded and moved out of the group again. She uncomfortably pulled a chair off of a table top and, shaking, placed it on the floor. She wanted to say that they should be nice to her. She wanted to tell them about what she had been through, that she had lost a friend only moments before. Instead, she played with her fingers, her mother's ring. She held Aster's necklace in the palm of her hand. It was warm with her heat. She studied her strange company.

The dismissive man was shorter than the rest, with cropped brown hair and similarly colored eyes. He wore a green army coat which did nothing to disguise his muscular build, and reminded Ceres of the type of guy she had loathed at Atkins—the ones obsessed with their bodies and disengaged with school, the ones that were there because their parents wanted to vacation in France.

The man called Jack looked over after the men had finished their conversation and came over to her.

"Thank you for at least acknowledging me," she said, somewhat sarcastically.

"You're welcome. Hey," he patted her shoulder, "sorry about Matthias, he doesn't take well to newcomers."

She shook it off. "It's no problem. I just thought I could tell you what I knew."

"You can tell me," Jack said quietly. He had kind eyes, deep blue and almost unnatural. His hair was jet black, the color that hers was when she had first dyed it.

He was tall like Bry and he was kind, so she told him almost everything.

"Sege sent the note," he said.

"You know him? How do you know him?" she said surprised.

"I know you, too. Sege and I were in the same class. I knew you looked familiar when I saw you in the store, that's why I did what I did."

"I don't know you," she said.

"Jack," he said holding out his hand. She didn't take it.

"I don't shake hands," she said. Jack didn't ask why.

"Okay…Sege contacted us when he was captured. They didn't let him out of their sights until he signed the contract and we had to meet secretly. The Foundation is everywhere you think it is, but it's in other places too. He sent the note to the prisoners to leave at 8 AM because he was going to set off the explosion at 8:15 AM. He figured they would be out of the tunnel by then."

"They didn't all go," she said. "Four of them stayed. And Bry and I…" she stopped. She didn't like hearing his name. It reminded her that he was gone now too. "Is Sege alive?" she asked.

"We don't know. We won't know."

"Ever?"

"We have to be okay with the idea that we may never know."

Ceres didn't buy it. She didn't think that a person had to be okay with not knowing.

"How long will you stay here?" she asked. "Until it's safe?"

"It won't be. The chemicals have made this entire place a disaster area. It's so toxic that we will risk our lives even opening that door. We'll go back to the safehouse."

Ceres didn't understand. "Sege seemed so environmentally friendly. It doesn't make sense that he would blow up those pesticides if they were going to destroy the city, and to endanger so many peoples' lives."

"It wasn't his plan, it was Matthias'," he seemed agitated.

"And you're okay with that?" she scolded.

Jack shook his head, "I didn't know what was going to happen. Matthias said that there would be enough of a distraction to get us out of the city undetected; he never said that he was going to turn it into a wasteland."

Ceres looked up at Matthias, who was standing across the room talking to the rest of his followers.

She stood up and sat back down.

Jack looked at her suspiciously and she stood up again, walked towards the group of people and said, "Hi, Matthias right?" She was shaking badly, but she didn't know if it was anger or if it was fear.

Matthias acknowledged that she had called him the right name. "What do you want?" he asked callously.

"I want to know why you thought it was okay to pollute the entire city. I want to know why you risked all of these people's lives," as she held her hand to the others in the room.

Matthias laughed a little. "You have no idea about anything. You don't know about the Foundation. You were just lucky to get out, lucky to find Jack."

Ceres was taken back only slightly. "I know plenty about the Foundation. I was on the inside. They hunted me like an animal and stole everything. Don't pretend like you have some kind of monopoly on information here."

"Why would they care about you?" he scoffed, eying her like Cane used to.

Ceres didn't hesitate. "Because I had heirloom seeds."

"Still have them?" Matthias asked.

She hesitated, "No."

Matthias was visibly annoyed. "We could have used those seeds. We could have used them to dethrone the mighty Foundation. Prom always says, 'people curse the man who keeps grain, but good for the guy who sells it.' We could've made him eat his words."

"I don't think that's what that means," Ceres murmured.

"Doesn't matter now," Matthias smirked. "You lost them. I hope you know what you've done."

Ceres threw up her hands. "You are bad. You are just as bad, if not worse, than the Foundation. There's no way for you to know how many people will be affected by *your* actions, but don't pretend like you're some saint that did something good for 'the people.' You aren't the people if you are willing to sacrifice them."

"For the greater good, girl," he said bitterly. "Don't pretend like you haven't made a huge mistake by letting them have those seeds, either."

"I didn't let them take anything," she said. She thought that perhaps she could have fought harder. She thought that she should have broken off an ear of corn before leaving the Foundation's greenhouse, but she hadn't thought about it, all she had thought about was how to get herself out, about Bry's body. Now the seeds really were gone and the onus for the reaping of growers across the country would be hers.

Matthias squinted his dark eyes at her, "Don't you know that those people knew exactly what they were getting into when they moved into the city? They moved directly into the outskirts of the world's food police. They paid for it with their taxes, their politicians were bought, and they knew that someday they would pay for doing nothing while the Foundation ruined the land, while they pumped it full of pesticides and their genetic anomalies. They got exactly what was coming to them."

Ceres heard Sege in his voice. Sege seemed mild mannered in contrast to Matthias, whose blond hair and grey eyes seemed more intense and more deadly.

A man walked into the room and said, "A car is here."

Just then, the seven of them collected their belongings and walked towards the door. Jack did the same and walked past Ceres as she watched them move out the first door.

Matthias looked back at her and then at Jack. "Come on," he said holding his arm.

"We can't just leave her here," Jack said softly.

"What difference is it between her and the rest of the people in the city? They have to make their own decisions, find their own salvation. And there isn't enough room in this car."

Jack thought about the seats and then stepped back. "You'll come back for the both of us then."

Matthias smirked, "You don't want to do that, Jack."

"Or we'll wait for the next car," he said moving back towards the table and sitting down. "It can't be far behind."

Matthias looked at Ceres again as if to say *his blood is on your hands now, too.*

The door slammed behind him and they could hear the roar of the engine though the walls.

"Why did you stay?" she said accusingly.

"I don't want to leave anyone behind. They'll send another car. Matthias won't leave me here." He pulled out a chair and sat down, folded his arms momentarily before chewing on the skin next to his fingernail.

Jack looked defeated and Ceres knew that he wasn't keen on what the group had done.

"If you didn't know, it's not your fault," she said.

"That's not any kind of logic," he came back. "Just because I didn't know means that I should have known. I should have been paying attention. I should have asked. Now, you're right, the whole city is destroyed and I was a part of the group that made that happen." He pushed his thumbs against the centers of his eyebrows and closed his eyes.

Ceres felt that she shouldn't be hard on him; she didn't know who he was, or what he was capable of.

"Are you from Epineio?" she asked. She felt as if she already knew so when he nodded, that she wasn't surprised.

"I thought that it was supposed to mean *safety.*"

"It does. It did? I don't really know what it means."

"Is it a place? What happens there?" she asked curiously.

Jack looked at her, guarded. "It's a place," he said stretching his neck from side to side, "a place that thinks of ways to crack the Foundation, so to speak."

Ceres looked around the nightclub. She didn't like his joke, or play on words, or whatever he had used to describe Epineio. She noticed that he looked uncomfortable and she wondered why he had stayed. She thought that maybe he was going to keep an eye on her, make sure that she stayed put until Matthias had a chance to come back. She wondered if he was some sort of psychopath that thought that this was his perfect chance to get a victim alone with him to enact his sick fantasies. She quickly dismissed both ideas when he knelt down to the ground and picked up a few pieces of broken glass from the floor. He must have genuinely been upset at his group for what they had done. She felt bad for questioning his intentions.

The walls of the club were a faded grey and next to the door that they had exited out of there was a full bar. She saw the restroom's blue and yellow door.

"I'm just going to go to the restroom," she said awkwardly, pointing to the door.

"Be my guest," he said throwing the glass away. "Be careful."

She thought about saying, 'Why? It's just a bathroom.' In her characteristically sarcastic way, but it seemed as though he was being sincere.

She could see why Jack would tell her to be safe in the grimy dirt of the nightclub bathroom. She looked into the mirror at her half-dried shirt; her jeans were still slightly damp from the sprinklers in the cellar, or the prison, or the hold; wherever she had been, before she'd lost Bry.

She went into one of the stalls and sat on the tank of the toilet with her feet on the seat. She stared into the unsavory condition of the toilet bowl and spit into it. She felt saliva form in the corners of her mouth. She thought for sure she was going to throw up again, this time it was for her miserable condition, not the toxic fumes permeating her body.

She held her hair behind her ears with both hands, anticipating what would come next and read the writing on the walls. One read, "Poets can turn nightmares into classical music" another, "Remember–you're alive. And that is sort of a miracle."

"Sort of a miracle," she mocked. "Completely a miracle."

Ceres thought that she would've seen Bry alive again by some sort of miracle. She used to think the same thing about her parents. She couldn't process the death. It was unreal to her. In Bry's case, she couldn't understand how he could've been coerced to eat, compelled to eat the corn. She was mad, angry. She didn't know what had come over him in the greenhouse. It was like he'd already given up, even though he knew they were on the way out.

She'd lost everything; Aster, Bry, the seeds. She leaned back against the wall of the restroom and held the pendant of Aster's necklace tightly in her hand. She leaned forward again, holding it in both hands and resting her chin on her knuckles.

She started to hum, she tried to remember the words to her mom's favorite hymn and sang, "*Come, thou Fount of every blessing, tune my heart to sing thy grace; streams of mercy, never ceasing, call for songs of loudest praise. Teach me some melodious sonnet, sung by flaming tongues above. Praise the mount! I'm fixed upon it, mount of thy redeeming love.*"

She hummed the same tune two more times, singing "redeeming love" at the end of each verse, then rested her forehead against her knuckles again.

She heard a *tink*, as in an opening. She felt her hands move only slightly. She pulled back her face to see that the golden box had opened, broken and cracked along the ridges. She was first entirely upset, only to discover that it was this way by design.

She pulled it open to reveal a blue seed, sprouting from trapped moisture inside.

"You didn't have to stay," she said when she returned, "I'm going to leave."

Jack was caught off guard, "Why? Where will you go?"

Ceres didn't know if she should tell him that she had the last chance to redeem herself hanging from her neck. She didn't know if he could be trusted. She didn't know if she should ever trust anyone again. She only knew that she should leave the nightclub before Matthias came back, if he ever would.

"I'm going to find a place. I don't want to go to Epineio."

Jack seemed to jump up out of his chair.

"I'll go with you, I don't want to go there either."

Ceres was skeptical of his behavior. "I don't know if you should come with me," she said.

Jack looked annoyed.

"I don't know if I can trust you," she said.

"Were we not in the same bookstore when I saved your life?" he asked.

Ceres took a deep breath. "Yes, but..."

"I think you should realize that I *just* gave up everything I knew so that you wouldn't have to be alone."

"I can be on my own," she replied.

"Okay. The least you can do is let me come with you so I don't have to be."

She realized that it was possible that *he needed her*, though she didn't need him. "Are you on my side?" she said.

"Yes," he replied. He looked directly in her eyes and she looked long enough that they began to look real.

"I have the last seed."

Ceres showed him the seedling in her necklace and then closed it again promptly.

"What are you going to do with it?" Jack questioned, "Sell it?"

"I don't think it's mine to sell. That's why I don't want to go with Matthias." She paused, "Whatever I do, I have to protect it. I can't risk it getting into the wrong hands."

"Won't it help people though? Won't it stop the dependence on the Foundation?"

Ceres shook her head. She didn't know. She thought maybe they *were* dangerous. They sat on the barstools and she started to spin around in her seat. "How much do you know about farming?" she asked. Bry had been her guide before.

He shook his head, "Not much. I know that corn, specifically, can cross-pollinate with other variations of corn to produce another species of corn entirely."

"Ya," she said, "that's what happened when Bry and I planted the corn in the first place, but it ended up bastardized by the other corn in the field."

"Did anyone try to eat that?" he asked.

"No, Sege did an experiment on it, that's how he knew that it was heirloom."

Jack's eyes widened. "Heirloom," he repeated. "That's probably why the body can't digest it properly, it's not used to an original form of the plant."

"So planting this really wouldn't help anyone. We'd make the seeds but we would have to train ourselves to eat it again."

"Maybe. That's a lofty task," he replied.

She nodded her head and jumped down off of the stool. There was a reason that she was entrusted with the seed. It was her purpose.

Ceres went behind the bar and collected items that she thought might be useful to them on their journey. Jack worked on ripping up a cloth to cover their faces as they ventured back outside. They would have to be exposed to the chemicals for a prolonged period of time if they were going to get out of the city, out of the cloud. There was no telling how long it would take for them to find a car, and when they did, they didn't know how long it would take for them to get out of the city. There must've been accidents all over the town.

In the city, it was protocol for anyone that was subject to a chemical spill or explosion to stay in their house or place of work when it happened. The panic lights went on throughout the streets. They were white blinking lights that flashed three times then stopped, then three times more with a dull hum and a high-pitched beep.

It was early enough in the morning that there wouldn't be too many people out and about. They said it was for the good of the city streets and for the safety of the city's people; it was a way to clean up their messes without anyone knowing or getting in the way.

Still, Ceres thought that it might be easier to get out of the city now, when there was a considerable amount of chaos, than to wait for the air to clear and risk detection.

Prom may have snuck away in the corridor they had escaped from in the moments before the blast, and if he did, he would know that she was alive and on the loose. She didn't know if that information would come back to haunt her.

They wrapped the masks around their faces, leaving only a slit for their eyes to see through. She tucked her necklace into the front small pocket of her jeans after wrapping it with plastic wrap from the bar. She had found some spectacles and some sunglasses in the office of the nightclub that they would use to hide their eyes from the elements. Ceres let Jack pick which ones he wanted and he picked the sunglasses. When they were finished wrapping their faces, they looked as if they were patients in a hospital or as if they had dressed up as mummies for Halloween. Ceres put on the spectacles, which were just for show, and Jack put on the backpack and sunglasses.

"Bummer," he said putting them on his face and tucking them into the mask.

"What?" she asked.

"These are prescription. Who would have thought that?" he laughed.

"Well," she said, "you picked'em. Ready?" She put her hand on the door.

"You follow me," she said sternly.

Ceres opened the door, and although they had tried to protect themselves from the air conditions, they could clearly smell the noxious odor of the area. Jack started coughing almost immediately and Ceres turned to him. "Hold your breath," she yelled through her mask.

She held her hand up over her nose and mouth to shelter it a little more from the substances that floated in the air around them. The air was a thick, oily vapor, and difficult to walk through. Ceres didn't know if it was genuinely difficult or if the idea of being trapped in a cloud of pesticides was clouding her outlook.

They ran down the empty alleyway to the main road and to the sidewalk. There were people lying on the pavement and in the middle of the street. Facedown, they convulsed in the fumes, coughing and holding anything they could over their faces.

Ceres couldn't believe that Sege wouldn't have thought about this, that he would have hurt all of these innocent people just because of his own hatred of the Foundation. It only reaffirmed her decision to leave, not to wait for Matthias or to go to Epineio, if he'd given the orders.

They tried all of the car doors on the street to see if they were open, to no avail. Ceres spotted a car with its driver's side open and no one inside. Apparently someone had tried to make a run for a shop or a door that would be safer than a car.

"There," she said pointing across the street. They ran past a few more cars with their drivers passed out inside and over to the car. Ceres jumped into the driver's seat and unlocked the doors for Jack, who hopped into the passenger side.

The keys were in the ignition and after Ceres fumbled with them, they departed.

"Do you think Sege is alive?" she said as she navigated slowly through the streets.

Jack looked over at her and pulled off his sunglasses, rubbing his eyes with the inside of his t-shirt. "I don't know. If he is, he'll go to Epineio. I don't know how he could have survived that explosion. It wasn't anything but fumes for us, but he was right by it," he said looking to where the Foundation used to stand. "The whole east side of the building is gone."

Ceres felt sad that Bry's body was probably lost forever under a pile of rubble and chemicals. She thought that he deserved a funeral, that she would have gone to it.

Jack explained how Sege sent the note and the key to the prisoners in the basement room. When Sege contacted Epineio, he told them that he had overheard a worker in the research lab talk about the exit that had been used as a ventilation system before the building made advancements in the last few years and stole the key they "irresponsibly" left unattended in a drawer.

Sege didn't know that he was carefully manipulated into thinking that his friends, whom he had heard would be placed in the room, would be able to safely escape his secretly planned blast the next day. He didn't know the exit, the ventilation system, had been renovated with the updates, as well. It had been fitted as a firebox, designed to give hope to those that wished to escape, and to squelch that hope in flames with the flip of a switch. He assumed that they would be safely in the streets, able to find shelter before he set off the disaster.

They weaved their way in and out of cars and bodies on the city roads. They entered into the area that Ceres had known well. She started to recognize the façades of the buildings and names of the streets. The high school was up ahead and on the outside of the town. She drove past it slower than she had the other buildings. Jack kept an eye out for Occa.

"Is it weird," he said, "that we walked these streets only a few years or so ago and we thought that the Foundation was just an office building with a park?"

Ceres nodded, "It's strange that it was right outside of our backdoor and we didn't know that we were actually just living in the shadow of it." Matthias's words rung in her ears, that they knew what they were doing when they moved into the city, that they were part of the problem.

She didn't want to be a part of the problem. She thought that Matthias was a part of the problem. The smog that they drove through was evidence. They passed the sleepy school dormitories and dining halls and no one peeked their heads outside. It was a ghost town.

As they approached the exit road, they saw men and women in biohazard suits checking out the cars that left the city. There were police cars on the perimeter, but there weren't any officers to be seen. Presumably, they had commissioned the Foundation to check the cars at the Foundation's suggestion. Perhaps it was just a façade, or perhaps they would say that they stayed in their cars while the police did all of the dirty work, looking for a fugitive. The presence of security indicated to Ceres that Prom was alive. Otherwise, they would have let people freely leave the city's chemical smolder.

"Doesn't seem like the time to make sure that people are who they say they are," Ceres said passing a car to her right and then turning around.

"Where are you going?" Jack asked.

Ceres veered through a stream of abandoned cars and a few panicked pedestrians. She just looked at him and smiled, memorizing the curves in the road as she went. She turned around, gaining speed as she went and barreled through the barrier on the northbound side of the road. Her foot pushed the gas pedal to the floor, and she could hear the car struggle to accelerate at 95 miles per hour, then up to 105.

Ceres held the wheel with white knuckles, checking her rearview mirror constantly.

"They're not following us," she said, flustered.

"Do you want them to?" he said trying to hide his fear. He held onto the handle on the top of the door tightly and managed to put on his seatbelt with his left hand.

"Oh, here they come," she said switching her eyes between the rearview mirror and the road ahead of her.

"Ceres, they will catch up to us and they will kill us."

There was no one else on the road except for their car and the police, who were a few miles behind. Ceres knew that, if she kept her speed, she might be able to keep the distance between them until she got into the hills, where she could maybe veer off the road to lose them. They wouldn't be able to see that she had done so; they would think that the car had flown over the next hill out of sight.

"Hold on tight," she said. She thought that she might have been crazy. But if she died in this way, it would be her own doing. She wouldn't die at the hands of anyone else.

She let up on the gas and then kicked it again, pushing the car into overdrive and forcing the gas light to go on as the fuel injectors sucked out all of the remaining fuel. They left the ground momentarily when they went over the hill, causing Jack's stomach to drop. She saw a gas station and a patch of trees and slowed down enough to swerve off the road and behind the station. She pushed both feet on the brake petal and they both lunged forward before swinging back again.

"Good thing you put on your seatbelt," she laughed.

He looked over at her, barely concealing his shock that she had been so reckless. He started to second guess his willingness to join her.

They turned around in their seats to see the flashing lights of the police cars fly by on the road behind them. Ceres ripped off the shredded cloth mask from her face and Jack followed. Ceres felt alive. She enjoyed it before realizing it might be dangerous to crave that kind of excitement.

Ceres looked at the back of the gas station at three gas cans lined up on the back of the building.

She unbuckled herself and hopped out of the car before running towards the cans and shaking them to see if they had any fuel. She struggled to hold two semi-full containers as she got back in. She thrust them at Jack as they fell from her arms.

Jack struggled to catch them and place them upright. "Think fast, Ceres. We have to go somewhere out of sight quick," he said.

A man came barreling though the parking lot from the gas station, swinging a rolled up news magazine in his hand. They could hear him screaming something about "damn kids" before following the road away from destruction.

Ceres turned up the radio and punched the buttons until they landed on a station with music.

"We can't listen to this," Jack said.

"Why not? It's classical. It's supposed to help soothe you," she replied.

"It is stressing me out," he said biting at his fingers.

She turned the radio off, "I don't want to stress you out," she muttered. "You shouldn't put your fingers in your mouth like that," she said and he shot her an embarrassed look. "It's really unsanitary."

Jack changed the subject back to the radio, "Just until we know what we are doing. We need a place to go. Any ideas?"

Ceres scratched her neck, then her arm. "We have to go somewhere with a shower. I don't think we should have this on our skin for very much longer."

"Agreed," he said opening the glove compartment. He pulled out a silver and black 9mm. "Well at least there's this."

"Let's not use that," she said quickly. A tremor ran down her spine at the sight of it. She motioned him to put it back into the glove compartment.

"Not a fan of guns?" he countered.

"Not a fan of all of these people dying. I don't want to have anything to do with anyone else dying."

Jack put the gun back in the glove compartment and took out the maps and booklets underneath.

"Well this is helpful," he said pulling out two hundred dollar bills from one of the envelopes.

"A gun and money. Suddenly I think we might have stolen the wrong person's car," she said.

"They couldn't be very good at what they did if they only had $200 in their glove compartment," he said back.

"See, if you bite your nails now you'll have gun and money germs in your mouth," she said, her voice sounded like her own mother's in her head.

He smiled a little, "Thanks, Mom, but I think the toxic chemicals we just ingested are a little more pressing."

"There's some pretty gross stuff on money," she replied. "I saw it on some documentary."

Jack laughed to himself at her concern. "I'll be alright."

They pulled over to a small store to figure out their next direction. Ceres stayed in the car while Jack went in to get water. She watched him as he walked, his back straight; she thought it was strange that his lack of slouch didn't seem unnatural like most.

When he jumped back into the car he asked, "This guy that died, Bry? Why did he die?"

Ceres thought. She was hesitant to answer, "He ate the corn. When they took the seeds from us, they grew them overnight and Bry was curious. Prom was there. I think he told him it was okay to eat. He ate from one of the ears in the greenhouse. There was something terrible in the air, a gas maybe…" her voice started to break at the end of her sentence.

"Love him?"

It bothered her that Jack talked about him so flippantly. "I don't know why people keep asking me that. Of course I love him. Loved him. Love him. Don't you have to love everyone that you care about? I love Sege, too. Does it matter that I love him or that I care that he is dead? I don't know. I don't know," she muttered. She pulled her bangs down over her eyes, trying to make them grow over her face again.

"I'm sorry. I didn't know. It seemed normal to ask and I shouldn't have," he looked at the map. "You said that they grew those seeds overnight, right?"

"Ya," she said picking the hole in her jeans, making the gap even larger. She remembered when it was just a threadbare section of her pants.

"Seems messed up that they want to feed the world and they don't share that technology, only the kind that they profit from."

"Money is everything," Ceres said, wondering why it wouldn't be satisfying enough to know people were no longer hungry. She thought that maybe their hunger for money caused the same gut-wrenching pain she had in her stomach at that moment from little food. It must have been a visceral pain, because it didn't make sense to be so reckless with people's lives unless it actually caused physical discomfort.

"It's also incredibly dirty," he added.

They decided to try Bunton, a town in the mountains of the next state over. They drove for hours. Once they'd passed state lines, they'd have to go north for 76 miles before seeing if they had made the right choice.

Before they made the turn north, Ceres noticed the cannery that Bry said Cane sold his corn to. The light was fluorescent but hardly noticeable in the midday sun. She saw a truck making a delivery and she could have sworn it was Cane's long hair and beat-up truck making the distribution. It was 3 PM and they hadn't stopped but once to fill the tank with two of the gas cans and get water.

Ceres was starting to fall into her delusion. How her entire life had changed in less than one full week escaped her. She had gone from the farm, whose comforts were great in contrast to the discomfort of the last 48 hours, to Sege's cabin, to the Foundation, to a nightclub, to a fugitive on the road for the second time. She hadn't really eaten in days. Her skin was dry and itching from the poisonous mist that had enveloped them in the city. She had lost, and then found, her companion; then he was lost again in what seemed like a sort of permanence.

She felt like she had replaced him with Jack and then the guilt flowed through her. She thought back to when she wanted to leave the farm. She didn't want to ruin Bry's life, and she didn't want him to lose it, either. She felt that if someone were watching her life, they would judge her for moving on so quickly, but she couldn't stop breathing just because he did.

They exited the freeway to Bunton and the road narrowed. Ceres had been driving while Jack had fallen in and out of sleep in the past few hours, but was now awake. He put the map back in the glove compartment.

"What now?" she said.

"I guess we should've been talking about that," he replied groggily.

"We have to get this off of our skin," she said pulling at her shirt. "It's going to get worse if we don't."

They drove slowly up and down the streets of the town. They were catawampus in their design. There were several areas where they hit dead ends and had to, awkwardly, make five-point turns in order to turn around in front of mothers watching their children.

Jack laughed at her driving skills and she cautioned him that she could do worse, so not to push her.

They saw a lone motel on the end of the town and pulled into the back of the lot, behind the green dumpster.

"We can't make this a permanent plan," she said. "If we only have $200, we'll have to figure out a way to make money to keep shelter. And food."

"And we need to plant that seed, right?" he said pointing to her pocket.

It was as if she had completely forgotten the reason why she was on the run, that she had a mission that needed to be completed.

They walked into the reception area, with a bell ringing behind them. The carpet was green and the accents were all gold. The desk in front of them was embossed with gold leaf and sported a pale pink counter.

A sweet-looking young lady got up off of her chair and put down her gossip magazine.

"Hi, y'all!" she smiled. "Welcome to the Mountainside Motel. How may I assist you today?" She sounded as if she was reading from a script, but her happiness was apparently sincere.

"We need a room," Ceres said. "Just for the night."

The young lady punched in a few things in the computer while the pair tried not to make eye contact. The girl kept looking up at them and making a face that made them wary.

"Everything okay?" Jack asked. "D'you have a room?"

"Yes, sir," she said. "It's just, your skin is red and looks like it hurts real bad. I'm so sorry. I shouldn'ta said anything. It's none of my business. Please excuse my discourtesy."

Jack rubbed his neck. "We'll keep it between me and you."

The girl smiled and handed them a key attached to a hole-punched guitar pick. "I'm Betta if you need anything."

"This is neat," Ceres said smiling at the guitar pick swinging under her palm.

"Thanks!" Betta smiled back and walked around the desk. "I'll help you with your…" She saw that they didn't have anything with them.

"In the car," Ceres smiled back. "Honey, will you go out to the car and get them?" she said putting her hand on Jack's shoulder.

Jack smiled back and said "Sure, *honey*."

Ceres walked to Room 8 on the second floor overlooking the parking lot. She saw Jack walking out to the car and she threw him the keys from the balcony.

Jack collected a gym bag from the back of the car and filled it with random items from the trunk to look like they had brought luggage with them. He turned to see the lady watching him over her magazine from the reception window.

Ceres had left the door to the room cracked and went to look at the state of her skin in the mirror. She had seen Jack's red neck, and the back of his hands with a rash of specks of white. Her case was only minor; there were some lines of red on her neck and chest. Her condition may not have been visible from the outside, but her lungs felt heavy. She had wanted to cough in the car; she wanted to cough then and there, but was afraid that if she started, she would never stop.

Jack walked in, shut and locked the door before he threw the sack on the bed.

"One bed, huh?" he said dryly.

"Don't get any ideas," she said "I didn't want to cause any more suspicion in that girl. She seemed to think we were strange customers."

"We are strange customers," he said dumping the bag. "I found a shirt and some gigantic pants in this guy's gym bag."

Ceres made a face.

"Don't judge. I'm going to take a shower and I'll go into town to see if I can't find something for you to wear."

She nodded. She thought it was nice.

He walked over to the bathroom and shut the door.

After Jack, Ceres took a shower in the small and blue shower tub. She let the water roll over her skin for a few minutes before she touched it with the body wash Jack had found in the gym bag. It smelled like a forest; it was not a distinctly manly smell. She felt like she was bathing in a pine scented candle. Her hands moved over her gritty skin. She slicked the water off of her body, trying to push as much of the pesticide off of her skin as possible.

She sat on the bed in a towel around her with another around her hair, waiting for Jack to come back from town. Her skin was relieved by the warm water rinsing away the chemicals from the surface, but it didn't seem to completely relieve the fog that she felt she was in. The locket was out on the table, still half opened with the pressure of the burgeoning seed.

She heard someone's footsteps on the landing outside. Her heart skipped a beat and she held tightly to the trigger of the black and silver gun she found in the gym bag.

She quickly threw it to the side when she saw Jack's face.

"Ah, now you're okay with the gun," he said smiling. His hair had dried in a shaggy mess on his head.

"I smelled those hideous, gigantic pants you're wearing, and I knew I should be scared."

"You should see what I bought you," he replied. He threw the plastic bag at the bed and placed a small terracotta plant holder on the table. "We'll use this until the plant gets bigger."

She nodded and took a deep breath. She sifted through the bag that Jack had tossed on the bed.

"These aren't so bad," she said turning around and putting on the clothes.

Jack caught himself staring at her bare back, the faded bruises on her arms.

"I went to a consignment store, spent $15 on the shirt and pants. $5 for everything else at the corner store. I figured you wouldn't want second-hand underwear," he said.

"You figured right; beggars can't be choosers though," she replied, turning around.

She picked up the bag and pulled out a pair of socks. "These for you?" she said throwing him a pair of jeans from the bottom of the bag.

"Ya, 50 cent special," he said. "I couldn't wear *these* any longer."

She laughed at him. "Do you feel alright? Your skin doesn't look much better."

He rubbed his neck with his hand. "I'm okay. I'm sure if I just drink a lot of water it'll go away."

"Should we see a doctor?"

"We only have $120 left, and I don't need a doctor. I'll just drink water and keep it clean. Let's just drop it, okay?"

Ceres did. She didn't want to push him. They should have seen doctors. They should've sought help— but she didn't know who was safe and who wasn't.

"I have to eat," she said. "Can we go?"

They walked down through the lobby to Betta and her magazine. She smiled and took her feet off the counter. "Ya'll have a good night!" she said loudly enough for her manager in the next room to hear.

The pair smiled back. "Any good place to eat close by?" Jack asked.

"Ya, Aileen's is two doors down on the right."

They walked to the diner on a path of pebbles and dirt. The smell of evergreens was overwhelming. Ceres felt like she was on a camping trip, like the ones she'd been on with her mom and dad, Aster and Erving. Cane hadn't ever come on those trips, and after spending the last few weeks with him, she was glad for it. It was easy for her to try to imagine she was somewhere else; lately, the changes hadn't stopped.

Aileen's was a little diner with checkered vinyl tablecloths, teal-colored outside and in. After they were were seated, it became obvious that they were the only people in the whole restaurant, save for an elderly couple eating soup and reading the paper.

Whenever Ceres saw someone watching the television, or reading the newspaper, she immediately felt unease. She didn't know if her face was plastered all over the broadcast. She knew if it was, the Foundation would lose credibility, so her bet was that they were only secretly alarming their people to her recent escape.

"You worried about the paper?" Jack asked reading the menu.

"A little. But if they wanted us to be on the news, they would have flashed our faces all over it by now. Besides, they already killed me off a few days ago," she said.

Ceres went over to the wire paper holder and grabbed the top copy to bring back to the table.

It was only four pages, front and back, *The Bunton Daily*. She read the headlines of lost puppies and school science fairs and her fear was assuaged. "We might have picked the right place to go."

The waitress was an older teenage girl, maybe having just graduated from high school. Ceres thought that she was college aged, but there was no college around. Ceres made up that she was probably stuck in the town until she could pay her way out.

"What can I get ya?" she said through chews of her gum.

"Water and…"

"Pancakes," Ceres interrupted. "Can we get the pancake special?"

The waitress gave her a funny look, "For dinner? You want pancakes?"

Ceres nodded.

"Pancakes for me, too," Jack added.

When the pancakes arrived, Ceres placed her hands on her lap and prayed. She stopped before saying "as it comes from God's green earth" because she didn't know.

"Why did you decide to come with me?" Ceres said between bites.

"What's for me there?" he responded. "They're just as criminal as those they try to protect people from."

Ceres nodded in agreement. "I wonder why Sege was so enamored with them, enough to do what he did."

Jake looked up through his shaggy black hair. He blinked his blue eyes a few times, as though he was trying to remember how he'd ended up with Sege and Matthias in the first place, "He was always at the coffee shop I worked at after I dropped out. He and Matthias were close. Matthias has a way with people. I'm not surprised he got Sege to do what he did."

"What do you mean he 'has a way with people'?" she asked.

Jack shrugged his shoulders. "He's persuasive. Maybe he's not. He just knows when people need something, someone, somewhere to belong. That's how he got me. He's got some kind of sixth sense for vagabonds."

"How was Sege a stray though? He was pretty well off. His parents adored him," she wasn't convinced.

"Listen," he said, "I just know that he's got a way with words. He tells you what you want to hear."

She wanted to ask him what it was that he had wanted to hear to get him to join Epineio, but she didn't. He took a drink of his water and she tried to change the subject. "Why'd you drop out?"

"Same reason I joined Epineio. I couldn't afford going to school at Atkins. My mom and dad were growers; they killed themselves sophomore year. They lost the farm and I had to provide for my little brother, Griffin, who lives with my grandma now. The Foundation forced them into bankruptcy. My parents didn't want to just hand over the keys to the place, so when they came to collect, they were found in their bed, having drank the same pesticides that the Foundation had delivered the days before." He said all of this in between ravenous bites of his pancakes. "I had gone to Atkins until then. Lived with my grandma and Griff and finished school in the public school system."

Ceres got the answer to the question she couldn't ask. She was horrified at the story and at Jack's lack of euphemisms. She didn't know what she was supposed to say so he just continued. "Griff looks exactly like me, only five years younger. That's why I came with you. I don't know why you would use chemicals to hurt people, or yourself." His voice trailed.

"I'm sorry about your parents," she said meekly.

"They're dead. They could have taken some action, but they didn't. It wasn't even on the news. Anyway, I was mad and Epineio said they were going to do something about the Foundation, so I joined ranks."

When the bill came, Jack slipped a twenty out of the envelope and handed it to Ceres.

"We're going to have to talk about money," Ceres said quietly. "I can get a job. Maybe I can work here."

"I'll have to work too. We can't spend $60 a night in a motel. Maybe we can sleep in the car. I don't think we can make $60 a day plus the money we need for food."

"You don't think we can make $60 a day between us? I think we can find something to pay at least that."

Ceres looked around at the dearth of customers in the diner. She wondered how much the girl made there. She calculated, at an average $4 tip, ten tables would only surmount $40. The girl may only get 10 tables a day and split between them, she'd only make $20 at most.

"We won't be able to whip out our resumes and demand $20 an hour, Ceres. Do you even have ID?" he asked.

She didn't. There was no record of her anywhere but in her own memory, her bag at the Foundation. She didn't know how she would live without a name.

"Let's pick out new names," she said with a glint in her eye.

"You go first. This oughta be rich," he said leaning back in his chair.

"So negative; you should go by Nelly. Negative Nelly."

"How about just Nell. Nelly sounds girly," he said with a frown.

"I'll be Demi," she smiled.

"Ok, Demi," he said getting up with their plastic bag of leftovers.

She chose the name because it was the name of her best friend as a child. She had always wanted to be her. She wanted her life, her clothes, her house. The least she could take now was her name.

Ceres asked for an application as she left. The girl said they didn't have applications, only jobs, and there was a shift open the next night. Ceres gloated that her part of the deal was done; it was Jack's turn to find employment without a social security number, though he said that he would have to wait until Monday.

On the way back to the motel, Ceres thought that Demi was probably on her way to pre-med by now, law school perhaps, she was always smart. Both of her parents were still alive. It made her sad that her own life was so different. She had never imagined her parents would die when she was so young. She had wanted them to be there when she got her first big job, her first promotion, a boyfriend and eventually when she got married and had children. She thought they would have liked Bry. She decided that she wouldn't be jealous now. She thought that everyone always wanted to make a difference; that they wanted to make a permanent footprint on the world. She shouldn't be angry that her footprint came early. Perhaps it would reach deeper into the earth than Demi's ever would.

As they approached the motel, Ceres veered towards their parked car and Jack followed. Ceres emptied the to-go bag and handed the Styrofoam containers to Jack. She knelt and started to dig into the ground until she found moister dirt. It was almost like clay. Jack knelt down to help her and they selected a mixture of wet and dry for their terracotta pot before heading upstairs.

They filled the pot three-quarters of the way with dirt before Ceres placed the corn seed in the container and covered it up again with the remaining soil.

"Here goes nothing," she said. She didn't see anyone drowning. She saw the dirt as real, as nutritious. She saw the seed swimming gracefully in the grains of dirt, finding its bearings.

"The chances of that one seed producing anything are really slim," Jack said abruptly.

"Some chance is better than *no chance*, Jack," she replied without looking at him.

"If it killed your friend, why are we making more?" Jack asked timidly. When he saw Ceres's face he immediately wanted to retract the statement.

"It has to be more than that; Aster wouldn't have given me something that was designed to kill people. She said 'let this be your food,' that has to mean something."

Jack pursed his lips together. "What if it doesn't mean anything?" he said. "What if they really are seeds that are too pure or too toxic to eat? Will you be okay with that? You'll have to be."

Ceres nodded and filled a glass from the desk with water from the tap to pour into the pot as Jack got into the bed.

He slept closest to the door, at her request, with the gun on the side table next to him. They were lying with their backs towards one another when Ceres turned to her back and said, "I'll go by Ceres."

He turned onto his back as well and pulled the sheet up to his face. "Then I'll go by Jack."

Ceres couldn't sleep for more than a few hours at a time. Every time she closed her eyes, she felt as if she was being chased, that she shouldn't be lying down, that she was stupid to close her eyes.

When she was a little girl, her mother had told her to pray when she was scared, but Ceres never prayed past 'please make this sadness go away.' Instead, she sang *Jesus loves me* in her head until she could fall asleep.

She got out of bed and went to the planter. She picked up the necklace in the darkness and felt her way around the clasp and the hook, placing it back on her neck.

When 8 AM came, Jack was still asleep and Ceres was sitting at the table with her seedling, eating the pancakes they had taken home in the Styrofoam container. The pancakes were warm and sticky from the moisture trapped inside the white walls. She looked over at Jack and wrote him a note.

The sun was bright that morning, and for some reason, she felt happier. She didn't know why; she was exhausted. Maybe it was the small amount of sleep, or the pancakes. She walked down the stairs to the dirt road and headed, again, past Aileen's. She smiled at the girl that they had seen the previous night. She came outside of the diner to tell her, "Shift starts at 4."

Ceres thanked her and kept walking. It was colder there than it had been on the farm, but warmer than it had been in the halls of the Foundation. It was a crisp morning and Ceres held her arms with her opposite hands, rubbing them up and down to get rid of goose bumps.

She turned left at the stop sign and went across the street where she saw a little congregation forming. She hadn't realized it was Sunday. There was a little white church tucked into the little town's foothill. It had a spire with a bell that rang as Ceres walked up to the gate. The pastor was at the front of the building, greeting the parishioners as they entered.

She stood next to the white cast iron gate and chipped off some of the paint where it had started to peel. She didn't want to just walk up through the doors; she waited for an invitation to come in, and she got it. "Come on up, miss," the pastor said waving his arm in a welcome. She smiled.

Ceres entered the white gate and looked up at the man who was standing at the top of the wooden stairs. He reached out and shook her hand.

"I'm not dressed for church," she said.

"Luckily, God doesn't care how you're dressed, just where you are dressed," he laughed and she smiled. "Pastor Brad. Sit anywhere you like," he said, as he followed her inside and left the door cracked behind them. She didn't tell him her name.

There were many vacant rows, but Ceres took one of the seats in the middle, on the outside. She looked around her to see an older group of people. She saw the couple that she had seen at the diner the night before.

The pastor took the podium at the front of the pews. He was a soft looking man with brown hair and eyes. He was wearing a suit and tie that looked like it was uncomfortable to him. He kept trying to loosen the pressure of his necktie with his hand. It may have been suspicious if he had been sweating, but it was not because he looked so kind.

He started with having everyone stand and greet one another; Ceres always hated his part of church. Some of the congregation struggled to stand but did anyway, greeting their friends with smiles and cupped handshakes. There was no one sitting next to Ceres, so she simply stood and smiled at the people who turned to look at her. She was the youngest there by far, the next youngest was probably one of the single men in their 40s or 50s. Ceres tried to make out if they were married, or widowed. She wondered why it mattered.

When she sat down, there was a new presence next to her. It was a woman, in her 30s or so, with short black hair and big silver hoop earrings. She sat in the seat directly next to Ceres, which made her wonder why she sat so close. There were so many other seats, *why would she choose this one?*

Ceres moved down the pew a little and sat down.

"Stand up everyone, let's sing!" Pastor Brad's voice rang out through the wooden walls.

Ceres heard the chords. They were familiar to her and she started to shake a little. She smiled. She warbled, "Come thou fount of every blessing" singing as if she was the only one listening. She felt that, somehow, *Bunton was always on her map.* She thought it could be an indication that she was in the right place, as if someone were telling her that it is all part of a plan, or part of her purpose. Or maybe it was her mother saying 'hello' and 'you're okay.'

When the song was over, the lady next to her reached out and covered Ceres's hand. She didn't like how uncomfortable it seemed. Ceres patted it and smiled, then pulled away and listened.

At the end of the service, Ceres sat on the pew past the time that everyone else had left, including the lady next to her. She leaned back and slouched down with the wood of the pew cold against the back of her neck. She closed her eyes to the sound of the emptiness in the church; said a prayer for Bry, the people who died underground in the Foundation. The silence was nice, though it was only for a moment.

"You sing?" she heard a lady's voice ask.

Ceres opened her eyes startled. "Only sometimes."

"It's nice. I'm Ann, Brad's wife."

Ceres was confused. "Hello Ann," she replied.

"We could use a voice like yours. Even being here is good, if you could just be here," she turned to see who was speaking; the lady that had been sitting next to her had reappeared.

"I don't know what you mean," she said.

The lady came and sat at the pew in front of her and turned sideways. "Or are you just travelling through?"

Ceres compressed her lips. "I hope not, I'm kind of sick of the…travel," she replied. "We're staying at the motel across the street and I don't think we can stay there much longer." She was surprised at her willingness to give honest answers.

"You and your husband?" Ceres didn't correct her. She wondered if she even looked old enough to be married. She played with her necklace. "You can stay with us if you'll help us out. As long as you need," Ann implored.

Ceres was skeptical of the offer. She wanted to ask why she wanted her there so badly.

"I feel like you should be here," Ann said. "We've been trying so hard to get some younger people here and it's like pulling teeth." She laughed. "Kids don't care about God anymore."

"A lot of people don't," Ceres said suddenly.

"Well, then you show up, and with that voice!" she smiled. Ceres found comfort in her compliment, her sweet face. Somehow she could see her mother there.

"Ask your husband, see what he thinks. It might be nice to stay in one place for a while."

*

Ceres happily walked back to the motel. She was sure that Jack would accept the invitation with alacrity. They would still have to make money for food and make a plan for the seed, but it was better than throwing $60 away for every night they stayed at the motel. She thought it was strange that Ann would assume she was married so young, but maybe that's what people did around here. She was sure Jack would be happy to go with the plan.

She walked back into the room with Jack pointing the gun directly in her face.

She jumped. "Seriously, Jack," she said angrily.

"Where have you been? I thought someone had taken you," he scolded.

"I left a note," she leaned over to the table and picked up the coffee stained paper.

"I thought they made you write a note and took you," he said putting the gun down.

"And I have the imagination," she said smiling. He bit the side of his fingernail again.

Jack went over to the door and locked it, then looked out the window.

"I went to church," she said.

"Why'd you waste your time?" he said callously.

"They offered us a place to stay," she said, taken aback by his aversion to the idea.

He looked directly at her and said, "What is the catch? Conversion? Who we selling our soul to here?"

Ceres sat on the chair next to her seedling.

"I can just go, if you are going to act like this," she said facetiously.

"You're suggesting we separate? Now? You going to go join some cult and I'll just hang out in this motel room until I run out of money?" She hadn't been serious about their separation at first, but now she considered it.

"All they want is for me to sing in their service, get some young people in the church."

"So you're going to start some kind of choir in the church? That is literally what this is, you know. Sister Act. Ceres's Act. Dumbest idea I've ever heard," he joked.

Ceres laughed at the idea of dressing as a nun. There were no habits at this church though, just a piano and a guitar. She thought it would make her mom proud; her dad always liked to hear her sing.

"It's a free place to stay until we have some money. You're in or you're out," she said collecting her clothes.

"That's a logical fallacy," he said, squinting his eyes. She rolled hers back at him. "I'm in," he conceded. "Sooner we get on our feet, the sooner we can figure out what we're going to do," he said.

Ceres hadn't thought about what the next step in her plan was and if Jack would only be a temporary companion.

A frazzled man with a crumpled up note sat fidgeting in a lab coat. He tapped his foot against the metal of the filing cabinet, creating a loud and echoing thud each time his foot hit the side. He heard the door open behind him, letting light into the dim laboratory.

"Mr. Holland, you've been requested," a woman's voice said. He turned his face to the side to see an outline of Mae standing in the hallway. She was alone, wearing a mask. "Mr. Holland," she said again. "I'd hurry if I were you."

"A minute, please?" he said in a frail and wobbly voice.

"Excuse me?" she asked, raising her voice.

"One minute, please!" he said again, this time louder and more angrily.

She shut the door. He got up and yanked off the sleeves of his lab coat to reveal the sweat stains on his light blue button up shirt. His hands trembled as they fumbled with the buttons, rarely done up to his neck. He wore horn-rimmed glasses. He fumbled with the filing cabinet next to his desk, first not fully compressing the button on the handle and swearing under his breath at the locked drawer when he pulled. He tried again and pulled out a yellow and green tie that didn't match his shirt in the slightest. It was already tied and clipped onto his shirt crookedly. He looked in a small mirror he had taken from the cabinet and placed on top of it. He straightened it as much as he could, rolled down his sleeves and buttoned them at the wrists.

He heard Mae knock at the door. "Mr. Holland!" she said loudly. "Your minute is not an hour!"

"One moment," he said, his voice cracking. He took his business jacket off of the coat rack by the side of his desk and patted it down for dust. When he put it on, he felt the cold of his sweat retouch his skin under his arms and he started to sweat even more.

He pulled a black comb out of the pen drawer in his desk and managed to comb down the mess of his jet black hair. He lined up his lab coat on the back of his chair and pulled out the shoulders so they weren't crinkled in. He brushed his hand across the back of the chair and patted it twice.

He took the crumpled up note from the desk and balled it in his pocket.

Mae reached to open the door and summon Mr. Holland one more time when he opened the door and shook her hand.

"Jep Holland," he said shaking vigorously.

She gave him a look as if she didn't care. "I know who you are, Mr. Holland."

He followed her down the hallway to the elevator. "I'm surprised you are at work today," she said. "We first looked for you at home, but your wife said that you had come in, like always. You must have such dedication to the Foundation."

"Yes, ma'am. My work is everything."

"Your work or your guilt," she said glibly.

"Guilt?" he said, his voice breaking again. "I have no guilt. Where are we going?"

"Oh, you'll see," she responded, looking back at him with a smile. The building had been fully ventilated, but she handed him a mask anyway. "You know what these chemicals can do to your body," she said.

"Yes, ma'am," he said taking the mask.

"They've cleared it from the hallways, but you know Prom, he likes precaution."

Mr. Holland made a face. He knew that Prom Dierts didn't like precaution, he loathed it. Perhaps she was talking about precaution when it came to his own personal safety. Either way, he had heard the fans and air cleaning crews all morning. He had even tested out the air himself before taking off his hazmat suit hours before.

They went into the elevator and Mae pushed the top button. Mr. Holland closed his eyes as his stomach dropped and the elevator blasted to the conference floor. He scrunched the note in his pocket, wishing he had destroyed it before he got in the elevator with Mae, burned it, or chewed it up and ate it. He thought about doing it now. He grasped the note, nearly tearing it in half with his fist. Before he could swiftly pull his hand from his coat pocket and shove the notebook paper in his mouth the elevator came to an abrupt and shocking stop.

"Explosion must have knocked some wire loose," she said smiling at him. "Remember that on your way back down."

Jep was happy that she alluded to the way down, even if it would be on a seemingly standard death elevator. The door opened six inches below the line up to the floor they stopped.

"Lovely," Mae said, stepping onto the carpeted hallway. Jep followed suit. He felt hot beads of sweat form at the temples of his hair. He pulled his hands out of his pockets and Mort met them at the doorway.

"Mr. Holland," he breathed in his ear as he passed.

"Nice to see you, Mork," he responded. Mort sneered at the misnomer and followed them into the conference room. Prom was standing at the window towards the back of the room. There was an easel with an empty white board sitting on it next to the table. The view to the outside showed a fierce blanket of cloud over the city below with teal blue sky above.

"Beautiful day, isn't it?" Prom said sarcastically as they entered.

"Um, yes sir," Jep replied.

Prom turned around, still with his hands held together behind his back. "It's not a beautiful day, Jep. It's a very un-beautiful day." His eyes were bloodshot and stressed. Jep could tell that he wasn't well.

"Have you been exposed?" Jep asked sincerely.

"We all have been, Mr. Holland," Prom stated. "Take a seat."

Mort led Jep to a seat at the table and practically pushed his shoulder down. A muffled "I was going to sit" was heard in the room.

"What happened yesterday was a tragedy, would you agree?" Prom began.

"Please sit down, Mr. Dierts. You look unwell," Mae said, pulling out a chair for her boss.

"Thank you dear," he said taking it.

Mae was short in her interactions. She was sick of cleaning up messes.

"Sit down, please, Mae. Relax for a minute," Prom said.

"There's that sarcasm you've grown so accustomed to in the last 24 hours," Mae said looking across the table at Jep, alluding to the mess he was.

Jep gave a frazzled smile to Mae.

"Well now that we're all here," Prom said leaning back in his chair. "Mr. Holland, do you know how this all started?"

Jep didn't know if he was talking about the Foundation or the meeting or the explosion.

"What, sir?" he replied, his voice shaking.

"When I was young, I was a bit of a prodigy," he laughed a little. "Now I don't want you to think that I'm full of myself. I really was a very intelligent little boy. But it was just me, my mother and my father on the farm and the farm is no place for a prodigy. You know what a prodigy is, right?"

Jep nodded and sweat began to leak into the fibers of his sport coat.

"At around 14 years of age, I had pet cat. Its name was Milo, which is a boy's name but I'm pretty sure that the cat was a female. It was an older cat and I wanted to take it in as my own to make sure that it was taken care of. It was always roaming around the farm so I just said it was mine. I don't know if it actually ever was. Either way, the cat would like to go out into the fields and scratch down the corn stalks before they could grow tall and vigorous. I tried to train him away from it, but he was already set in his ways. There was nothing I could do."

"That's not good," Jep interrupted. Prom gave him a look to let him know he wasn't to interrupt again.

"At the time, my father had spent the majority of his time coddling the corn fields. It was our cash crop. So naturally I feared for the cat, knowing that something terrible would happen to it if I didn't take care of it myself. My father was so angry, screaming at the heavens, saying that he would string poor Milo up by his tail and let the birds peck out his intestines. It was a horrible image. The cat caused a greater divide between my already strained parents. So one night, I went out in the darkness of the fields, after my mother and father had gone to sleep. I walked around for ages, hours. It took everything I had to keep my eyes open, and even then, the thought of having to get up early the next morning to help on the fields was heavy on my mind. Eventually, I heard the soft purr of the cat in the shed with the rest of the animals. Do you know what is going to happen, Jep?"

Jep shook his head. He didn't know if he wanted to know.

"I had, in my back pocket, my pillowcase from my very own bed." Jep started to feel increasing discomfort.

"I knelt down to the sweet little cat and scooped him up with my very own hands, placing him inside the pillowcase, which I can tell you was where the niceties ended. Cats aren't particularly fond of being placed in small places. I suffocated him, in my very own pillowcase." Jep was horrified. "Once he stopped struggling, I pulled him out of the case and took his limp body behind the shed and buried it. Then I went back to the farmhouse, put my pillowcase back on my pillow and went to sleep. I no longer had to hear my father scream, or my mother shout about money. Instead, I just did my work. Do you know why?"

Jep looked him square in the eye. "Because you didn't want your father to get a hold of him?"

Prom smiled with his mouth and his eyes. "Yes! You are quite smart. I knew that whatever my father would do was going to be twenty times worse than suffocating my sweet little Milo in the pillowcase. It had to be done. For Milo."

They sat in silence. Jep wondered what the point of the sadistic story was.

"I started out the story telling you I was a prodigy. A very smart child," Prom continued. "I was naturally smart, intuitive. There weren't many things that I couldn't figure out and most importantly, I was, and still am, a critical thinker, a problem solver."

Prom leaned against the grains of the shiny conference room table. "Do you know what ammonium nitrate is?"

"NH4NO3, sir. It is the main ingredient in our pesticide products."

"And you know this because you helped refine and create our products, yes?"

"Yes, sir. I did help to do that," he stammered.

"100 tons of ammonium nitrate were ignited yesterday morning," he paused. "You are a very smart individual, Mr. Holland. You graduated at the top of your class. You are always first on campus, last off campus. You are a highly valued chemist here. You created the technology to detect cross-pollination signals; a very important aspect of our business model going forward."

"Thank you, Mr. Dierts. I enjoy working here."

"Your son, on the other hand, did not like working here so much, would you agree?"

Jep started to squeeze his hands together tightly under the table. "No, sir. I would say that he did not."

"And yet, we forced him into the research program anyway. In a very short time, he made me realize what a great mistake it was. A grave mistake, even. You see, Sege is like Milo. He is a roamer. He is smart, a genius even. Much like his father in many ways. And just like Milo, he liked to be free. Milo was a wild animal; he was never meant to be tamed. I shouldn't have tried. But when I realized that he couldn't be an asset to me or my family anymore, I eliminated him. Partly out of greed, because I knew that the farm would someday be mine but not if it went under, and partly out of pity. If my father would have gotten a hold of the animal before I did, I would say that Milo would have been brought to a very painful and unfair end."

Jep only partly understood the analogy. "What exactly do you want me to do? Exactly?" he squinted his eyes a little. "I haven't heard from him, really, since he's been here. How do you know he's even alive?"

Mae breathed out deeply and dropped her pen on the table. "We didn't find his body in the debris. He isn't dead. You know this though, I think. You eliminate the problem or we will. He will not leave this building or this city. He cannot."

"Either you suffocate him in a pillowcase or we'll string him up by his tail," Mort said sharply. "We're sure he'll contact you." He smiled a sinister smile from the corner of the table.

Jep shook his head. "I can't do that. Couldn't, I mean," He took off his glasses and rubbed the bead of sweat that had fallen through his bushy eyebrows out of his eye.

"You have a choice. You always have a choice," Prom said. "In the meantime, back to that 100 tons of ammonium nitrate. Someone is going to need to be called to the carpet for that. We have Sege on surveillance, setting up the explosion, then nothing. It disappears. He disappears. The media knows it was Epineio, but we didn't have appropriate safety precautions in place, or so it seems. Heads are going to need to roll, and publically. Several people have died and wouldn't have, save for the attack by your genius boy."

"I can do it; I can do anything you ask. I just can't hurt my boy," Jep said frantically.

Prom smiled. "Mae, brief Mr. Holland on the protocol." He leaned over the table as he stood up. "Jep, is it really hurting your boy if you save him from me?"

Ceres and Jack were at the church by noon; they had left the car at the motel until they knew it was okay to bring it. There was no one at the church anymore.

Ceres knocked on the church door with the pot tightly in her other arm. Nothing. She didn't dare look back at Jack. She already knew what his face looked like. She knocked again, pulling her wrist back farther to make her blow louder.

She heard the creak of the wood floor from inside and waited for the door to open. It was an older man with a shock of white hair and not much else. He eyed them up and down.

"Church is over," he said, and shut the door.

She heard Jack say, "How welcoming." But she didn't turn around. Ceres knocked again and the man opened the door again.

"We were invited by Pastor Brad and his wife."

"Round the back, yellow house," and the door shut again.

"That was a creepy mother…"

"Come on, Jack. He wasn't that bad," she said walking back down the path.

The yellow house had white eaves and an ornate white door. The grass was green and the trees were fenced off by little white wires that curled and bent in beautiful ways. Ceres thought it looked like a perfect doll house. Before they could make it up the walk, Ann had opened the door and walked out onto the wrap-around porch.

"I'm so happy you made it!" she said beaming. They smiled back. "Where are your things?"

"This is it," Ceres said indicating the pot. Jack held up the plastic bag.

Ann frowned. She wanted to ask why they didn't have anything else. "We have lunch ready inside," she said, feigning joy.

Ceres suddenly didn't know if this was the best decision. She remembered that she had told Ann that she and Jack were married and forgotten to tell Jack. There was no time now as they walked into the house and into the foyer.

"Does this need washing?" she said to Jack indicating the bag.

Jack nodded, then thought again about the chemicals on the clothes. "I think actually that we might just throw them out."

"Then you just have the clothes on your backs?" she asked.

Ceres looked down, embarrassed and then nodded.

Jack and Ceres sat at the kitchen table while they heard Brad and Ann speak in the other room. Ceres grabbed Jack's hand.

"I told them we were married."

"What? What was the purpose of that?"

"I actually didn't say we were married. She said it and I didn't correct her. I think they wanted to help us because we were a young couple."

"A *really* young couple," Jack snapped. "So you lied to the pastor and his wife. You can't feel good about that," he replied. Ceres wanted to tell Jack that he was being miserable. His demeanor had changed as soon as she had mentioned the church. He'd been so cynical, so negative, it was becoming depressing. Suddenly, she missed Bry. She thought that he would have loved Brad and Ann. She didn't say anything about it to Jack. She remembered what it was like to be told that everything was going to be okay after everything that she had been through with her parents and she didn't appreciate it. She had wanted to be negative then, so she let him be now.

Ann and Brad walked into the room. Ann stood slightly behind Brad, who was now dressed in a blue shirt and khaki pants. Brad could see their unease, so he sat down across from Jack and Ann, pulled out the chair and sat in front of Ceres.

"We're happy to have you stay here," Brad said, shaking Jack's hand.

"Thank you, sir," he said back. Ceres was happy that he was cordial. She felt a responsibility for him and embarrassment when he was rude.

"We just have a few questions for you," he said, holding his hands in front of him on the table. He played with his wedding ring. Ceres took her hands off the table to hide their lack of adornment and quickly pulled her mother's ring from her right hand and placed it on her left.

"We need to know if you are criminals."

Ceres's stomach dropped. "No, sir." Jack responded. They were, Ceres thought. Perhaps they weren't. Maybe it wasn't really a lie. It was more subjective.

"We would like to know how you came to be in this predicament," Brad continued softly. "You don't have to tell us everything, if you don't want to. We just want to know how we can help."

Ceres didn't know how to answer that question. She didn't know what she needed, or what could help. They couldn't provide any of the answers that she was looking for. The answers that she needed were at the Foundation and she didn't know how much of that was left.

"Are you growing drugs in that pot?" Ann blurted into the silence.

Ceres pulled the pot into her chest from the top of the table. "No," she almost laughed. "Actually, that is the one thing that we need. I need to grow this seed in this pot."

Brad and Ann were dumbfounded at the request. It was clear that it was strange that that was the only thing they would ask for.

"And a place to stay, until it grows maybe," Jack added.

"Let's make a little arrangement," Brad said nicely, "You two can stay here until the plant grows."

Ceres and Jack waited for the other end of the deal.

"What do you think?" Ann said sympathetically.

"What's the other part? What's our end?" Jack asked.

"Well, Jack, you'll grow your seed and Ceres might sing at church a little. Maybe you can get some young people to see church isn't so bad."

"That's it?" Ceres asked.

"Don't forget to show hospitality to strangers, by doing so, some people have shown hospitality to angels without knowing it," he said.

"Is that from the Bible or something?" Jack asked.

Ceres stomach dropped further at the assertion. She thought perhaps the offer would disappear if they knew that Jack wasn't too keen on God.

"Yes it is, Jack. Maybe when your wife here sings, you'll hear a few things you like in the sermon," Ann chimed.

Jack smirked. "Yes, I do love to hear my *wife* sing."

Ann took Ceres upstairs to the second floor of the Victorian house to show her where they would be staying. She opened one of the doors to a dark room and then turned to look at Ceres.

"That'll be too dark. No window in that room," she said preemptively, and they continued down the hall. "This room here on the right is ours, but this one," she said opening the door to the left, "might just be perfect." She swung open the door to reveal a bright room with a glass door leading to a balcony. There was a four poster bed on the right wall that stood high off of the ground and looked like it had been fitted with clouds to lie on. Everything was yellow and white. There was a mirrored armoire on the other side of the room that Ceres went up to and looked inside at its empty cedar walls.

"This is too much," Ceres said.

"This is nothing," Ann replied rubbing Ceres's arm in comfort. "We'll give anything we've been given to help anyone we can."

"Thank you," she replied. "I can put my plant on the floor over here by the door; it's really perfect."

"What's in it? Can I ask?" Ann said.

"It's just something I want to see grow," she said.

"Seems pretty important" Ann smiled, the creases of her eyes showing her age.

"It might be," she replied.

Ceres went to the diner at 4 PM and Jack worked out a plan for a job with Brad. They felt safe. Ceres felt safe enough that she walked alone. When she arrived, she was handed a tip book, pen and a pink apron with ruffled edges that would've been worn in the 1970s.

As she worked the bar tables of the diner, a man asked for Channel 3. After some fumbling with the remote, she landed on the national newscast. A man in a dark grey suit and serious hair cut started to speak severely into the camera:

Authorities are pleading for those who have been affected by the toxic cloud to come to the Foundation for immediate treatment. Seventeen people have died. The earlier you are treated for your exposure the better. Miranda, back to you.

Thanks Don, I'm here with Prom Dierts, Founder of the Foundation with an exclusive report of what happened yesterday. Mr. Dierts...

Ceres looked up from wiping down the table to the face on the screen. It was the man they had made a statue of in the garden and the man who had offered Bry the poisonous corn in the greenhouse. He looked untouched by the madness of the previous day.

Hello, Miranda.

Mr. Dierts, what part did the Foundation play in the explosion yesterday? What caused the explosion that killed 17 and left thousands in respiratory distress?

Ceres saw the bar roll across the bottom of the screen. Seventeen names. Not one of them was Bry's. Maybe it was because they had already said that he died. While she watched, the man put his coffee cup out at the end of his extended arm, "Hey, lady. Service please."

We believe that a group called Epineio masterminded the event. We believe that when we caught the pair trying to blow up the Foundation a few days ago, it exacerbated their desire to do something drastic to our great company, our great community.

Prom took his eyes which seemed to be searing into Miranda and looked directly into the camera.

To that group, wherever they are…we will find you. You will pay for what you've done to the great community you destroyed yesterday.

Ceres changed the channel to a Western from behind the counter, and the man hardly noticed, watching the TV while he slurped his soup and dipped his crackers.

A older lady sat down at the bar to the right.

"What can I get you, miss?" Ceres asked.

"Oh, just a coffee, dear," she replied. As Ceres poured the kettle, the lady smiled. "You look so familiar," she said, trying to figure out where she had seen her face before. "Have you been here long?"

"Not long," Ceres said nervously. "Just today." She put the coffee down on the counter in front of her.

"I think I must know you from somewhere," she said flinging her purse over her shoulder and onto the counter at the same time. The coffee mug flew off the counter at Ceres and scalded her hands.

Ceres screamed and then winced. The lady sat quietly. "Oh dear," she said finally.

Ceres ran over to the sink and held her hands under the cold water. She squeezed her hands into fists violently trying to quell the burn. Then, abruptly, she felt a relief, but not the kind she was looking for. As she looked down at her left hand, her mother's ring had snapped on the thin gold band, right next to the hand that was holding onto the crowned heart in the design.

"Everything alright up there?" she heard a cook say from the back.

"Yes," she whimpered. She poured the lady another cup of coffee before wiping the tear that rolled from her eye.

On the way home, Ceres held $23 in her burned hand and the idea that Bry made 18 names. She thought that maybe Sege was part of that number too. Marta, her savior, would make 20. She was in her head too much to realize that someone was following her. She turned at the church, a quarter mile away, before she heard the footsteps tap on the sidewalk behind her. She started walking faster. Was it Mae? Cane? Mort or Ladybelle? Maybe it was a new threat. Maybe she shouldn't have been walking alone in a strange and sleepy town. Finally, she decided to turnaround quickly to see a yellow dog, following her, panting.

"Hey, puppy," she said relieved, and patted his head. "Go home."

She started again to the stop sign and turned left to head to Brad and Ann's house. She turned around again and the dog stopped and raised his arm, pawing the air.

"Go home, puppy. I can't take you home." She leaned down to see that he didn't have a collar on. When she was down near him, he placed his paw on her shoulder and pushed up on it to lick her cheek.

Ceres got up and walked to the house. The dog sat where she had left him and remained there when Ceres turned to the sidewalk up to the house. He sat under the streetlight, wagging his tail. She walked up the drive and into the house.

Ceres went into the house to see Jack, Brad, and Ann playing Chinese checkers in the living room to the left. She joined them as they sat on the floor around the coffee table and drank hot chocolate.

They sat far away from one another. They didn't joke or embrace. Ceres looked miserable because of her hand, but Ann thought it was for Jack. Ann observed them carefully to see any hint of intimacy and was unconvinced that she would ever find one.

In their bedroom, Ceres placed the broken ring on her nightstand and sat on the edge of the bed.

"Bad night at work?" Jack asked.

Ceres nodded and turned to show him her hands. "A lady spilled her coffee and I broke my mom's ring."

"Let me see," he said holding out his hands. She gingerly placed her hands in his and winced a little again.

"Most of the sting is gone now," she said.

"And you probably won't feel it at all tomorrow," he said back. "When I was 14, Griff and I were making macaroni and cheese. He asked if I would hold the colander while he drained the noodles." Ceres could tell what was coming. "When he started to pour out the noodles, his hand slipped and the water fell on my hands before I was able to move out of the way. It's the worst feeling."

She smiled a little. "I'm more upset about my ring," she said.

"It's just a thing," Jack said climbing into bed. "Things come and go. Your body can at least fix itself."

The next morning, Ceres agreed to help Ann in the yard while Jack went to look for a job and Brad offered to drive him around.

Ceres was out the front door first to see the yellow dog lying quietly, waiting. Ceres bent down and the dog rolled over on his back so that she would rub his stomach.

Ann came out shortly after. "Find a friend?"

"He followed me home last night," she said scratching his head as he stood up. She rubbed in between his eyes like she used to do to Dally.

"He must want you to be his," she said.

"I can't ask you to take in another stray," Ceres said, laughing.

"You can. But you didn't ask. I'm just telling you that he looks like he chose you. It would be a shame to let him down."

Ceres named the dog Howdy because he made her happy. He would sleep on the bed in between her and Jack, which made her comfortable because he acted as a living barrier. She didn't mind Jack, and she didn't mind that they were acting like they were married, but behind the doors they wouldn't be married. She couldn't find it in her to marry her soul to anyone. She felt like she had lost herself in the rubble of the Foundation. She felt if she loved Jack, or let herself, she would be losing whatever bit of Bry she had left.

She was angry about Bry, and about everyone else that she had loved. Because that wasn't in her control, the death; she decided that her heart could be the only thing that she could govern.

When Ceres and Jack were at work, Ann filled their armoire with clothing from the local thrift store. She felt like Ann was some sort of fairy, fulfilling wishes, outfitting her new friends. She had to guess their sizes and what kind of clothing she thought that they'd like.

Ceres discovered the gifts in the armoire during her nightly check of the closet. She remembered that Brad had said they might be entertaining angels when they entertained strangers. She thought that Ann was the angel.

Over the next few weeks, Ceres worked at the diner and saved around $300. Jack worked at a construction site across town. The foreman went to church with them and did Brad a favor by hiring him, paying him under the table, and by not caring that he didn't have a Social Security Card.

Ceres sang at the church every Sunday, at the request of Ann and Brad. She would sing with an older member who played the guitar, or sometimes she would attempt to play the piano and accompany herself. A few young people came in, though they were mainly people that Ceres worked with at the diner. It took a while for Brad and Ann to realize that it would take a lot more than the power of peer pressure to get people to join the church; they would have to meet them where they were.

Once after Ceres came home from her shift at the diner, she found Ann sitting on the couch in the front sitting room. She looked sad and miserable. Ceres sat down and asked if everything was ok.

"Yes, Ceres. I am just worried about your relationship with Jack," she explained.

The idea made Ceres uncomfortable in a few ways. She was angry that Ann thought it was any of her business, and this coupled with the fact that she wasn't really married to Jack and had lied to Ann and Brad.

"How so?" was the only way that she could reply.

"I'm just worried that being here isn't good for your relationship," she continued. "You don't seem like you are happy; you seem like you are acquaintances more than spouses. Brad agrees with me."

Ceres was careful with what she said. "We are fine. Just going through a rough patch." She felt the lie come out of her mouth. It was only a half lie. Or maybe it was just based in a lie. Or maybe it just seemed like a lie because it wasn't telling the whole truth. Ceres didn't know how else to respond.

"I just want you to be happy, together," she said.

At dinner, Ceres begrudgingly held Jack's hand during prayer and kept holding it on top of the table throughout the entire dinner, at least until her palms became sweaty.

Jack didn't ask what she was doing; rather he viewed it as an invitation to further the affection by putting his arm around her as they went upstairs to bed. Ceres didn't say anything, or correct the behavior. She thought that maybe she should accept it in the same way that she accepted the responsibility of the seed.

After they had shut the light off, Jack asked, "What do you think about suicide?"

She didn't know how to answer the question. "I think I wouldn't do it," she replied honestly.

"I mean, what do you think God thinks about suicide." There was a long quiet while Ceres thought, so Jack continued, "When I went into my parents' bedroom, after they had died, Dad held the Bible on his chest, my mom had her hand over it. I just think that..." he stopped and stared at the wall.

"I think that they did what they thought was their only option." It was her best answer.

"And God? What does he say about it? That they're in hell? They were good people, Ceres." She could tell that anything she said wouldn't be enough. She put her hand on his shoulder. "It's just hard to believe in something that tells you good people don't make it just because of one decision."

Ceres took her hand and pulled the blankets under her chin. "I don't know, Jack."

Ceres felt an overwhelming feeling of sadness push into her rib cage. It was the same sort of feeling she had

had when Aster died, when Cane had attacked her. It was pressing on her chest. She could only identify it as her heart hurting. There were always too many unanswered questions, too many problems. She thought about when life had been so much easier, how easy it was to not know what was wrong with the world. If given the chance, she didn't know if she would go back or if she was better off knowing.

"My parents are dead too," she said softly. He rolled over and looked at her. She didn't like the look on his face. She thought, perhaps, she shouldn't have shared the information; that he was the one who was sad and she somehow stole his sadness.

"Is that why you ended up with your aunt?" he asked.

Ceres nodded. "I just graduated. I'm not eighteen yet, so the court appointed my aunt and uncle as legal guardians." She stopped then began again, "Right before my mom died, she said that I needed to find Aster, that she would take care of me. I didn't think anything of it, cause I still had my dad. But then my dad died too, and he told me the same thing. He said, 'Aster will shelter you'." Ceres looked like she suddenly knew something she hadn't known before.

"What did you just realize?" he asked.

"When Aster gave me the seeds, she said, 'Let this be your food'."

Jack shook his head like he didn't understand.

"Maybe they knew that Aster had the seeds. Maybe they knew this was my purpose all along."

Jack smiled a little. "I don't know, Ceres. Does it matter what they wanted you to do, or what you should do?"

Ceres scrunched her face. "Can't they be the same?" She waited for him to say that she had to be okay with not knowing, but he didn't say it this time.

"I'll say a prayer for your parents," she whispered, closing her eyes.

"Ok," he replied. "I don't believe in that stuff though."

Ceres's eyes popped open again. "Good thing we aren't really married," she said sternly.

"Why?"

"Because we don't believe the same thing."

Jack scrunched his face a little. "What if I loved you? What if we loved each other? That's not enough?"

Ceres quickly said, "No," then didn't know if she actually meant it.

"Why?" he said just as quickly back.

"Because." Ceres wasn't sure if she really *knew* the answer.

"That's no answer," he laughed.

"I just think you have to believe the same thing," she said, again closing her eyes.

"Then I guess it's good we aren't really married," he chuckled as he shut his. Ceres didn't know why it hurt her feelings that he had said the same thing she had said moments before.

In the weeks that followed, she thought less and less about the past, about Bry or Cane, until she was reminded by the corn in the window. The stalk was growing wildly and when the tassel showed up on the top of the plant, Ceres shook it so it would pollinate the flourishing corn below.

She'd picked up a book on growing your own garden in the town's 50-book library. She was surprised the book was there, and it only had a short paragraph on corn. It piqued her interest in other types of gardening, so she asked Ann if she would be interested in starting a small garden at the back of the house. Ann agreed and said that it would be nice to see the plants grow.

They planted basil, beets and summer squash. Ceres told Ann that the basil reminded her of her aunt. She would pinch off the new growth every day and smell her hands for hours afterwards. She thought about the wreath she'd placed on Aster's head and wished that she could be near her again somehow. She would ask Aster why she gave her the seeds. She would ask her where she got them from, and who she was protecting them from. She wondered if she was doing the right thing. She wondered if she was growing poison. She assumed that she was. Either Aster didn't know what she had, or Ceres didn't.

Ceres was surprised when Jack suggested a game night for the church to encourage a younger congregation. He did it as more of a *thank you* for their hospitality than a real effort to get more people involved in the church.

Ann bought Ceres a blue dress that looked like she came straight out of the 1950s. She liked it. She found it in her armoire when she came home from her morning shift before the party. Ann was becoming something of a holiday surprise like Santa Claus or the Easter Bunny. The dress fit her perfectly with a heart shaped neckline. Aster's necklace hung delicately on her collarbone. After she put it on, she twirled around in it, allowing the air to pick it up and she felt girly.

She thought of the explosion, the chase, the blood, and the dead. She thought that a woman wearing this dress would never be put in that situation. She wondered what it would be like to never have to deal with the corrupt and depraved pieces of her life.

When Jack came to the room he looked at Ceres with wide eyes. He hadn't seen her look so nice.

"I'll go so you can get dressed," she said leaving the room.

"No wait," he said going to his nightstand. He opened the drawer as she stood waiting by the door. He turned around with the soldered gold ring and held it out to her.

"Jack," she quietly said taking it. "When did you do this?"

"Happy birthday," he said. "I figured we can't really celebrate it here and I saw we had the tools at work. I thought you might want to wear it again."

She slipped it on her finger, briefly thought about putting the heart facing inwards, and looked at it before holding her hand to her heart. She moved towards him and hugged him briefly. "Thank you," she said. "You don't know what this means to me." She pulled back and kissed him on the cheek before hurriedly leaving the room.

Jack and Brad led the games while Ann and Ceres greeted the guests. The basement of the church was decorated with twisted crepe paper streamers and white Chinese lanterns that Ceres had picked out. Had the lights been turned down, it would have been a romantic scene, but they were not. There were several students from the local high school there. The man who had greeted them the first time they had tried to find Ann and Brad was there too. He was the church's janitor with crazy white caterpillar eyebrows and a hunched over posture. He scolded the teenagers with his glare when they filled their punch cups too high.

"Don't spill!" he would warble from behind them. His concern was not unmerited. The carpet in the basement of the church was tan and easily mussed.

Jack wore a pair of black pants with a baby blue shirt that complemented Ceres's dress. When a song came on that Jack knew, he pulled Ceres over to him and started to dance with her. It was an upbeat song that Jack knew well enough to sing badly in her ear.

"Putting on a show for our church parents?" she said, as he picked her up and swayed. She fell backwards and forwards with his weight. He kept pulling up her arms and shaking them, telling her to just let him lead. They laughed and danced until he pulled her close and kissed her. Then he pulled away and she gave a small smile.

"That's enough," she whispered in his ear and excused herself.

She went upstairs to the sanctuary and sat at the piano while the music played downstairs. It had all been too much and she didn't know what to think, or to feel.

Jack wasn't far behind. She didn't look at him while he made his way around the piano and told her to "scooch."

She moved over and let him sit in the middle of the piano. His fingers found their keys and he played a slow and sad song. Ceres watched in awe that he could have hidden such a talent from her.

When he was finished he said, "It's the only song I know."

"I like it," she replied. "Does it have any words?"

"It doesn't need any."

In the morning, Ceres let the sun wake her up. She liked the way that the rays flickered through the grown corn plant. The top of the stalk had headed towards the window, growing sidelong towards the light. The leaves all but pressed themselves against the glass, stretching their veins to take in as much of the sun as possible. Ceres felt that this plant, this one, would have reached to the heavens had she let it, if she hadn't caged it indoors. She thought about replanting it outside, but didn't think it would make a second transplant. She couldn't risk the cross-pollination, or the Foundation tracking it somehow.

She sat up. Jack was already gone. She pulled his pillow into her body; it was still warm to the touch. She patted Howdy on the head and pressed her feet against the cold wooden floors of the room. She looked at the gigantic plant in the window, herself in the mirror of the armoire. Her hair was brown again. Her bangs had grown out and she was able to shove them behind her ears. She looked like herself, but different. She saw the remnants of the cut that Alta had given her. She had grown to like it. Scars belonged to people that had been through the extraordinary, the unthinkable. Her scars were physical just as much as they were emotional, and she liked that. They were the physical manifestation.

When it was time, when they were ready, the top of the silk had turned from a light yellow to a dark brown, the same way they had been when she and Bry had discovered their hybrid. She took the ear in her hand and pulled it down, twisting it with her hands. She sat at the desk and pulled off the silk. It wasn't as wet and mushy as the corn that they had planted. It was smooth and felt like real silk. She pulled it down, row by row to see the cerulean blue kernels of the corn. They were like little gems that looked like they held the universe in them. They looked delightful. Ceres husked the corn and put it down on the table to get the second one. She had to get the chair to reach it and, as she pulled it over and stepped up on the seat, she heard a cough, like an animal trying to clear a hairball.

She turned suddenly to see Howdy chewing voraciously on the corn. She screamed silently, "No, no, no, no, no!" and scurried over to him.

She tried to pull the corn from his mouth and he resisted, pulling his head away from her and looking at her angrily, as if she was trying to take away his only meal. She pulled at it again and he growled and snarled. She pulled the cob and his teeth shaved the middle from its precious stones. She let go; the damage had already been done. If the small amount that Bry ate had killed him, the dog would surely be dead within minutes. At first she thought that he should have known better. She surrendered and let him enjoy it.

She sat on the floor cross-legged next to him. She stroked his fur from his head to his tail in repetitious, fluid movements. She let him finish the entire cob as he devoured each milky kernel with his fangs.

She sat there for what seemed like forever. When he was done gnawing on the cob, he got up off the floor and passed her. He went and sat next to the plant and pawed at the pot holder. She didn't understand and she didn't get up. She watched him jump up and dance on his hind legs in front of the plant. He circled it and then came back and licked her face, then went to circle the pot again.

She wrote everything down. She wrote about the pesticides, the seeds, Aster. She wrote about Cane and the farm. She wrote about Sege and Epineio. She wrote what she knew about the explosion at the Foundation. She wrote about the Foundation. She wrote about Mort and Ladybelle. She wrote about Mae and the Occa. She wrote about the hospital rooms and the prison in the basement of the Foundation. She wrote about the exit behind the stove and she tried to remember as many names as she could of the people who died there. She wrote about Marta then erased it. She wrote about Jack. She wrote that he wasn't to blame for the lie or untruth that they were married and for him to do *everything he could.*

She asked for a funeral, if they could afford it. She asked if they would go. She said that she didn't need to be buried, but she would like to be remembered.

She told them what to do when they found her. She said to destroy all of the seeds; they were no one's burden but her own and they should be removed from the earth if they weren't going to help people. She said to not eat them. She said that *this is what happens when you do.*

For Jack she left a small note. She scribbled:

I am convinced that neither death / life, angels / demons, present / future, nor any powers, height / depth, or anything else in all creation, will be able to separate us from the love of God.- Romans 8:38-39

She wanted to say that his parents were in heaven, but she had no idea if they were or not. She didn't know if *she* would be or not, either, and she had to be okay with not knowing.

Ceres went to the armoire and pulled out the clothes that she had come into town with. Ann hadn't thrown them away; she'd cleaned them of their chemicals, and put them in the bottom drawer. Ceres knew they were there, but didn't want to wear them anymore, until now.

She put them on. She brushed her hair and placed it behind her ears. Then, she climbed on top of the chair and twisted and pulled the second of three cobs.

Howdy wouldn't leave her alone. He jumped up on her sniffing incessantly. He pawed at her legs until they felt raw from his nails. She went over to the door to the hallway and opened it to shoo Howdy out. She folded the letter that she had written and placed it in her back pocket with the folded Bible verses.

She thought about her parents greeting her in heaven.

As she pulled down the silk of the second cob, she heard Howdy's nose press against the door. She could see his shadow under it. He had flattened himself against the door as if he could make himself small enough to slide underneath it.

She thought about taking only a small amount to see if she could train her body to eat it. She took a breath. She pulled away the remaining silk of the plant. She sunk her teeth into the blue seeds. Her teeth broke their skin and they spurted out. Ceres thought that it was wonderful, like nothing she had ever tasted before. It was sweet and sugary. She had wanted to eat more, but after the first bite, she was second guessing her decision. She heard Howdy paw at the door again and thought that *he* was fine. She took another bite before she lost her thoughts and fell to the ground.

*

Ceres thought that, against the Foundation, she and Bry were nothing; she and Jack were nothing. The Foundation had been around for years, collecting assets and technology; none of them stood a chance. They never really knew what they were doing with the seeds, only that they were important. In the end, it didn't really matter why they were important, what mattered was that people knew they existed, that there was hope for a future without the ever-present presence of the Foundation. Maybe the seeds weren't the answer, but something was. And there were people looking for an answer. Some of them were good, like Jack, and some of them were not. But there were people who cared, who weren't apathetic to the series of injustices that were continually placed on the growers and the people who ate the growers' food. That was all that mattered, that people cared.

The Foundation had visited Cane, months before, to let him know that his niece and farmhand had been caught and terminated for threats to the Foundation. They wouldn't be returning. Cane felt relieved that the onus for their capture was no longer on him, but he felt a small amount of sadness at the death. He'd find more help in the next few days, after spending a good amount of time in town.

Sege had made it out of the Foundation with his father's help. He had hidden in the same vented system he had instructed his friends from Epineio to escape from. He had to crawl over their charred and desiccated bodies, all the while knowing that he unknowingly was the one who instructed them to go towards their deaths. At the end of the vent was an exit to the city and Jep met his son there. It hadn't even crossed Jep Holland's mind to turn in his son; he loved him too much. He knew that he would probably pay for his actions, but no job was worth more to him than his family.

Howdy scurried down the hall as soon as he heard Ceres's body hit the ground. The corn rolled to the door. Ann wasn't home. Brad was out in the garden. Ceres's face was smooshed against the wood panels. Her body had gracefully fallen across the floor. She would have liked the look of it, if someone were to take a picture from above. Though, her face was not graceful. Her mouth was open and there was a small pool of saliva forming on the ground around her face.

Moments later, perhaps it was hours, maybe days, Ceres's eyes fluttered open. She saw the ruffled skirt of the bed. She saw dust balls roll back and forth at the air vent. She looked up at the corn cob that had rolled to the floor and saw that she had really eaten from it.

There was a knock at the door. She got up quickly. She was surprised at how she felt. She felt strong, not sick. She didn't feel recently poisoned.

"Hello?" Brad said. "Ceres? Are you okay? Howdy's been barking non-stop."

Ceres looked into the mirror of the armoire at her face. She made sure that she was really there. "I'm fine, I'll be out in a minute, Brad. Thanks." She picked up the corn from the floor and heard him walk back down the hallway.

She inspected the corn. She wanted to eat more of it.

She went back to the mirror and examined her face closely. She looked at the color of her eyes. She touched the edges of the scar underneath her eye and she knew.

She reached up and took the last corn cob off of the plant. She twisted it in her hand. She knew what she had, and she knew what she was going to do with it.

Matthew 14:30-31

“But when he saw the wind, he was afraid, and beginning to sink he cried out, ‘Lord, save me.’ Jesus immediately reached out his hand and took hold of him, saying to him, ‘O you of little faith, why did you doubt?’”

When Ceres finally left the room, she wanted to find Jack. Part of her wanted to gloat in the fact that the seeds did mean something, that they were going to change the world. The other, stronger, part of her just wanted to share her joy with him; maybe it would make him believe in miracles, purpose.

It seemed like hours passed as she sat on the porch of the old Victorian. Howdy wouldn't leave her alone. He would force his nose and snout under her arms to try and get to the cob, sniffing incessantly into her skin, snorting when he didn't get what he wanted. Ceres thought it was funny to watch. She wanted to pull down the husk of the plant herself, but didn't dare to. She didn't know if sitting in the wind would allow the Foundation to pick up any sort of cross pollination signals or crazy kinds of pollen from the sole remaining kernels. She had to protect them, now more than ever.

When Jack came walking up the street that evening, Ceres could hardly contain her excitement. Her leg tapped against the deck of the front porch and her heart raced a million miles per minute. She didn't know if it was happiness or fear.

When he came around the corner of the gate, she sprang up and ran down the pathway to him, throwing her arms around his neck and nearly shouting. "The corn is good! The seeds are good!"

Jack just laughed a little and put one of his hands around her waist to hold her.

"What do you mean, Ceres? You didn't eat it, did you?"

"Ugh," Ceres said in a huff. "Can't you be excited? They are something! They won't kill anyone."

Jack looked at her disapprovingly. "Let's go inside."

Ceres followed him up the rest of the sidewalk to the house. She was annoyed, again, by Jack's negative attitude. *Yes,* the seeds could have killed her, but they didn't.

Ann and Brad sat together on the sofa in the entryway.

"Good evening," Brad said folding down his paper.

"Hello," Jack said back.

"Hi," Ceres hurried along after him.

"Strangest couple," Ann whispered as they went upstairs.

Jack put his jacket on the bed and Ceres shut the door on Howdy's face.

"Look Jack," she said pulling out the corn cob. "Look! We made something and it's real."

Jack just sat on the bed. He wiped his brow with his palm. He smiled a small smile.

"Good," he finally said.

"Good?" she replied, maddened. "Just good? This could solve everyone's problems. We can produce this, lots of this," she said shaking the cob in the air. "We can parcel it out; give it to farmers, save them from the Foundation."

"I get it. That's great," he said, his expression was blank.

"No, I don't think you do, Jack. This is a miracle. This is what everything has been about. This is why I was given the seeds, why we came here, why all of this happened."

"No, Ceres, I don't think you get it," Jack replied. "You're all I have."

"What?" she said, furrowing her brow.

"You're it. I've got nothing but you now."

Ceres lowered her gaze. She didn't realize. She thought of his parents. She couldn't think of anything to say. "You are all I have," she said in like fashion.

"Me and those seeds," he said soberly.

"Yes. You and these seeds."

"We'll need a place to plant them," Jack said. "And I don't know much about how."

"Neither do I," Ceres said. "But if we can make this one, we can make more."

Ceres and Jack told Ann and Brad the truth about everything. They didn't want to put them in danger, but they felt like they had a right to know. At first, they seemed disappointed in the lie, but after a while, it seemed as if they realized why they had done it. "Not that that makes it okay to lie," Brad would say in his preacher's voice.

Ann and Brad had some land, up on the mountainside that they gave to the faux couple. Ceres was grateful that she didn't have to pretend anymore, but she would still have to sing at church on Sundays, indefinitely.

After they had enough, they dried the kernels of the last cob with Ann's help. She had also had an aunt who lived on a farm and had spent several summers learning about how they used to save seeds.

The next spring they planted rows and rows of corn in the back lot of the mountain home. Some grew to the height of the window corn, others were squatted plants that hid in the shadows of the goliaths.

Ceres would walk the rows daily, impatiently looking for the husks to dry and peel back so she could pick them. She was often castigated by Jack, who would catch her trying to peel down the husk of the corn plant to see if the milky white kernels had turned cerulean blue, ruby red and bright yellow. They kept up large white barriers on the property, so that no one could see in and no pollen would make its way out. Jack crafted them from special plastic sheets so that the sun could still make its way in. No one was close by, so no one was suspect.

After they had enough seeds, they parceled them in lots of seven; one of each color of the rainbow. Ceres typed a note for each of the small burlap sacks.

Heirloom Corn it read. *Grow them, save their seeds. You don't have to follow The Foundation anymore. 'Gen. 1:29 Then God said, "I give you every seed-bearing plant on the face of the whole earth and every tree that has fruit with seed in it. They will be yours for food.' xCD.*

Jack was in charge of sending them out. They had met some like-minded people in the year since they made their home on the mountainside. They were surprised to know that there were so many people willing to stand up to the Foundation, in whatever way possible. He would tell them where they should drive and they would deliver each little packet into black mailboxes.

Eventually the Foundation would come for them. Eventually Prom, or Ladybelle or Mort would show up at their door. They knew that their days without conflict were limited, but it didn't matter. They did what they needed to do without harming anyone else, because it was right and it was truthful and everyone should have a choice.

Acknowledgements

I wish to extend a rather large thank you to the following individuals, without whom this book would not have been written: Tasia VanderVegt, for reading every version and not only dreaming of, but creating a better world; Dr. Judy St. John, without whom I would have resorted to writing about vampires; the late Dr. Jake Adam York, who told me to write; Sarah Warner, for helping to hone the manuscript into something readable; Haley Sisco at Warner Literary Group for her support; Dodie Ownes at the *School Library Journal* Teen Newsletter who believed in the manuscript and gave many wonderful and helpful suggestions; my wonderfully amazing parents and sisters who always believe in their kooky, sometimes overly enthusiastic, youngest; Kylan, for loving to play outside; and to my incredible husband, who must find my burgeoning fervor endearing.

About the Author

Kate Muus is a mother, writer, wife, college teacher, advocate for suicide prevention, pop-culture fanatic, daughter, sister, friend—not in that order. She has an MFA in creative writing from the University of Colorado, Boulder, and teaches English composition and philosophy to medical students in Aurora, Colorado. *Secret of the Seeds* is her first novel.